The Adventure of Charlotte Europa Golderton

A New Sherlock Holmes Mystery

Note to Readers:

Your enjoyment of this new Sherlock Holmes mystery will be enhanced by re-reading the original story that inspired this one –

The Adventure of Charles Augustus Milverton.

It has been appended and may be found in the back portion of this book.

The Adventure of Charlotte Europa Golderton

A New Sherlock Holmes Mystery

Craig Stephen Copland

Published by:

Conservative Growth Inc.
3104 30th Avenue, Suite 427
Vernon, British Columbia, Canada
V1T 9M9

Cover design by Rita Toews
ISBN-: 9781983657993

Dedication

To the scholars, scientists, and archeologists from many nations who have labored, usually in obscurity, to unearth, expose, and explain the wonders of the ancient historical places and periods of Western Civilization.

Dear Reader:

You can have your name in print.

Would you like to be a character in a future New Sherlock Holmes Mystery? I will use your name for: a hero (other than Holmes or Watson), a heroine, a victim (Careful on this one. You might not survive), a police inspector, a secondary bad guy, a secondary good guy, a servant or other minor character.

If you do, then send me your name as you want it to appear and the type of character you would like to be to: CraigStephenCopland@gmail.com and I will let you know when you are going to appear.

AND

Do you want to receive notice of each New Sherlock Holmes Mystery when it is published? And hear about all free and discounted books?

Yes? Then please do any or all of the following:

Follow me on Bookbub here:

www.bookbub.com/profile/craig-stephen-copland?list=author_books

Follow "Craig Stephen Copland" and "New Sherlock Holmes Mysteries" on Facebook

Follow me on Amazon Author Central here:

amzn.to/2JOJVvt

Warm regards,

CSC

Acknowledgments

My special thanks goes to Dr. Peter Stephenson of Michigan, an expert in the field of cyber-crime and a supportive and encouraging reader of my stories. He made the invaluable suggestion of using a conspiracy with the telegraph system as a Victorian forerunner of today's cyber-crime and gave several excellent ideas for incorporating it into the plot.

As always, I must acknowledge the great debt of gratitude to Arthur Conan Doyle. Of course, if you are a true Sherlockian, then the debt is owed to Dr. John H. Watson, who so diligently recorded his adventures with Sherlock Holmes. All of my stories are written as tributes to the parallel stories in the Canon.

This story is also a tribute to the era of *noir* mysteries and particularly to the genius of Dashiell Hammett.

I wrote this story while living in the Okanagan Valley of British Columbia and must note my thanks to the Vernon Writers Group who reviewed the early draft and made wonderfully helpful suggestions. They and my invaluable beta readers have been incredibly helpful and encouraging.

My best friend and partner, Mary Engelking, and my big brother, Dr. James Copland, read all of my drafts and suggest corrections, improvements, and necessary cuts. Yet again, I am thankful.

Contents

Chapter One
Miss Ruth Naomi Lightowlers

The incidents that I am about to impart took place in London quite recently. Under normal circumstances, when similar events occurred and would have placed a heavy burden on those involved should the public become informed, I have delayed, sometimes for years, or obscured their identities. In this case, I have done neither. My reasons are simply that most of the principals of the case, other than Sherlock Holmes, myself, and the good men of Scotland Yard, are either dead or in prison. Those still living might object to having their stories made public on the grounds that modesty inhibits their wishing the world to know of their bravery and heroism. But such recognition is their due.

On the other hand, there is a moral imperative that the public be made aware of some of the dangers that became apparent as a result of Holmes's solving of this highly intricate case. I am not suggesting that Sherlock Holmes and I are entering the realm of moral crusaders that was led for so long and so well by the great Charles Dickens. Far from it. But the citizens of Britain and abroad need to be ever vigilant that the fine institutions in which we place our trust—in this case, the Royal Mail—can become the instrument used by the forces of criminality and evil. To adapt a well know phrase, *caveat lector*.

The events began on a Saturday afternoon of the second week of January, in the early years of the new century. My dear wife was on a visit to America to consult with the women in that country who were leading the crusade for universal suffrage and temperance. As I often did whilst she was away from home, I moved back in temporarily to 221B Baker Street. In part, this was because of my affection for my friend, Sherlock Holmes but, I confess, it was as much or more my desire to have my needs attended to by the great-hearted Mrs. Hudson.

"Holmes," I said, as I pushed back after a delectable meal, "the sun is shining, and I have a mind to take myself for a brisk walk whilst you read and smoke the afternoon away."

He looked up at me, quite startled.

"Oh no. Please, Watson, do stay here. I was counting on your presence."

"For what possible reason?"

"This afternoon, I have three appointments. Every one of them is a woman. The fair sex is your department, and I was hoping that you would be present to make sure that I conduct myself appropriately."

His familiar long face and deep-set eyes conveyed such an innocent look of need that I could not say no. I smiled, retired to my familiar chair by the hearth, and after adding another log to the fire, sat back and relaxed.

"When does your first client arrive?" I asked.

"She is scheduled to be here in ten minutes, but that could mean anytime in the next half-hour. She is, after all, a woman."

I gave my friend a bit of a look of disapproval at his attitude toward one-half of the human race. Mind you, I did not disagree with him.

Exactly ten minutes later, the bell on Baker Street rang, and Mrs. Hudson descended the stairs to greet our visitor. She returned to us moments later and handed Holmes a slip of paper.

"The lady does not have a card," she said, "but she gave me this name."

Holmes looked at it and handed it to me. In a refined handwriting it read:

Ruth Naomi Lightowlers (Miss)

"Please, Mrs. Hudson, kindly show her up," said Holmes.

Our dear landlady did not move.

"I shall do that, Mr. Holmes," she said. "But I must warn you that she appears to be terribly distraught as well as highly attractive. Just the type for whom you have a hopeless weakness for waiving your fee."

Holmes feigned a look of mock surprise and smiled. He looked over at me and gave a sheepish shrug as Mrs. Hudson departed.

"Do I truly do that?"

"From time to time."

We stood to welcome our visitor. All I can say is that Mrs. Hudson's appraisal of her was understated. The woman who entered the room was beautiful; stunningly beautiful. She was not particularly young—I would have placed her approaching thirty—but she had a perfect alabaster complexion and a singularly attractive face. Long ringlets of her rich, red hair hung down and bobbed sensuously as she moved. Mrs. Hudson had taken her simple frock coat, but a dark tam hat, of the Parisian style, sat jauntily on her head. Her figure, accentuated by an inexpensive, tightly fitting black dress, would have given Botticelli's Venus cause for envy. The only aspect of her being that marred her perfection were her lovely green eyes. As Mrs. Hudson had noticed, they were somewhat swollen and reddened from a recent bout of tears.

She took a few hesitant steps into the room, stopped, and gave an imploring look at Holmes.

"Mr. Sherlock Holmes?"

"I am indeed, Miss Lightowlers. Please, do come in and be seated. A spot of tea, perhaps, to help you compose yourself?"

"Oh, sir. That would be very nice. The cab ride was quite unsettling."

"Mrs. Hudson," said Holmes. "Would you mind bringing our guest a cup? A little added fortification might be in order."

As Mrs. Hudson turned to depart, she gave me a look that seemed to say, *See what I mean.* I nodded back to her.

"My dear young lady," began Holmes, "you must be chilled from the winter weather. Warm up by the fire and enjoy your tea. There is no rush. Compose yourself, and we shall get to your concerns in due time." He stepped over to the hearth and placed yet another log on the fire.

"Thank you, sir. You are very thoughtful," she replied. Then she waited, saying nothing until the adulterated tea had arrived and she had consumed several sips. Then she dabbed her eyes with her handkerchief, lowered her head, and spoke.

"Thank you, Mr. Holmes, for agreeing to see me. I have nowhere else to turn, and I am horribly worried. In all honesty, Mr. Holmes. I am terrified."

"I can see that you are in great distress. Permit me to suggest that before telling us about what has upset you so deeply, just begin by introducing yourself and imparting to us a few details about who you are and your history. It is always good to get to know a client before plunging into the depths of a case. Relax, a few more sips of tea, and then proceed when you are ready."

I could not recall Holmes's ever having been so solicitous. His standard practice was to dispense with any social graces and brusquely tell the client to "State your case."

She did indeed take several more sips and then, in a dulcet voice, began.

"My name is Ruth Naomi Lightowlers, as you know. My family once came from County Connemara but have been living here in London since I was a young child. My father passed away nearly twenty years ago, and I have lived with my mother in Islington until recently. She has been, of necessity, very strong in spirit although somewhat weak physically and has not been able to earn much of an income. She takes in laundry, sewing, and mending work from time to time, but it pays a pittance. Since I was a young girl, I have earned enough money to support us both. I had to quit my schooling early, but I taught myself to type and take shorthand and have managed to secure a series of secretarial contracts from various firms in the City."

"Forgive me," said Holmes, "for interrupting. But why did you not seek reliable continuing employment? It would have provided far greater security."

"Oh, yes, Mr. Holmes, it would. I am not sure how to express myself in answering you. It is a somewhat embarrassing matter."

"I assure you that Dr. Watson and I are no strangers to matters that are delicate and confidential. We are here to help, not to judge."

The young woman looked up, wiped her eyes again and forced a smile.

"Sir, I have been both blessed and cursed with a physical appearance that men seem to be attracted to. I learned, soon after I entered work in the City, that if I were to stay too long in the same firm, one or more of the men would begin to make passes at me. The young ones claimed they wish to marry me, and the older, married ones, hinted at immoral arrangements. Young or old, it was obvious that their intentions were less than honorable and I wanted none of that. All I ever wanted was to have a quiet, peaceful life with enough money to support myself and my mother. I prayed that God would show me a worthy young man with prospects who might want me as his helpmeet for life and mother to his children. I recently met a man who professed his love and commitment to me, but he breached his promise. I am still praying."

"And no doubt Providence will indeed provide in its own time," said Holmes. "However, I am sure that you did not come here for my help in finding a husband, so please take another good swallow of Mrs. Hudson's tea and tell me why you are so upset."

She forced a smile, displaying a gleaming and perfectly aligned set of teeth. Then, after, draining her cup and pouring herself another, she carried on.

"Thank you, Mr. Holmes. Your kindness and understanding have made me feel much better already. My reason for coming concerns my mother."

"Yes. You said you lived together until recently. You have since moved out and live on your own?"

"I have," she said. "That was what led to the current concern. I said that my mother had a strong spirit. I have to confess that I must have inherited her fiery Irish temper. She was not at all pleased when I took my own room in a go-down on Wamer Street in Clerkenwell. It was only a few blocks from her, and I continued to visit her twice, sometimes thrice a week. Then, four months ago, I received an offer to do work for a prestigious firm that was setting up an office in Europe. The billet they offered was at a rate of pay several times greater than what I had been earning, and they would provide me a pied-à-terre in Paris and travel on the Continent. It was a dream come true, but my mother would not hear of it. She scolded me, warning that I would be an innocent abroad and taken advantage of and it could ruin my reputation. We exchanged harsh words, and I took the offer and went over to Europe. I dutifully sent a note or card off to her every evening, assuring her that I was safe and living a most circumspect life. She sent several letters back that were quite forceful, which I fully expected. But then ... but then, the letters stopped coming. For the entire last two months that I was there, I heard nothing. I could not imagine what had happened. I wrote letters and sent telegrams to her neighbors, and two of them wrote back that they had not seen her around recently. One of them even went to her flat and knocked on her door, but there was no answer. As soon as I returned to London, I raced up to Islington. She was gone. Her flat was undisturbed. All of her clothes and belongings were there in place. But she had vanished.

"I asked the neighbors, but they knew nothing. I reported it to the police, and they took down her particulars, but they said to me, 'Frankly, Miss, we have many more serious things to look after than a middle-aged woman who has taken herself on a bit of a holiday.' That's what they said. Well, I continued searching for her for several more days, becoming more and more upset. I shared my worries with one of my closest friends, and she said that I should come and talk to Sherlock Holmes. She had read those stories in the Strand about how you solve so many crimes. I told her that it sounded like a good idea, but that I had nowhere near the means to be hiring a famous detective. Well, she told me to go anyway. No harm in asking, she said.

"So here I am, Mr. Holmes. I have nowhere else to turn. I really do not know what else to do. In my heart, I know that something has happened to my mother and that I was the cause of it. You just have to help me find her."

Again, she was using her handkerchief to dab her eyes as she haltingly spoke these final words. Holmes reached his long arms across to her and placed his hands over the hand of hers that was not holding her handkerchief.

"There, there, my dear'" he said. "I am sure your mother is just fine, and I vouchsafe to you that I shall not rest until she is found." He sat back and continued, again in an unusually soothing voice. "Please give me some facts about your mother. Tell me anything that might be useful in helping me find her. And do not suppose that any detail is too small."

Miss Lightowlers smiled wanly and opened her handbag.

"Here is a small photograph of her. I take it with me wherever I go. Does that help?"

"That is very useful. And her full name?"

"Oh, yes, of course. How foolish of me not to have stated that already. Her name is Charlotte Golderton."

She then went on to describe her missing mother in some detail. Holmes sat and listened most attentively, nodding sagely at each detail.

"Your mother's name is not the same as yours," he observed.

"That is correct, Mr. Holmes. After my father died, my mother remarried. It was ... it was a mistake is all I can say. They were not happy. He was not a good man either to my mother or to me. He did things ... terrible things that were unforgivable. Fortunately, he deserted us after five years, and we were much happier with him gone. My mother is still legally married to him and has retained her married name. I might also add that of late she has been spending some time with a man named Lloyd Sunday. He is the man who so discourteously made promises to me and then violated them. I suspect that their friendship is not beyond reproach. Please, sir, do not ask me to speak of these matters again. It is painful and humiliating for me to do so."

I suspected that Holmes, true to form, was about to do exactly opposite of what she asked and so I intervened with an altogether unrelated question.

"Pardon me, Miss Lightowlers," I said when she had reached an end of her recitation. "As a doctor, I could not help but notice that the skin on the back of your neck is giving you some problems. Would you like me to take a look at it and suggest some sort of remedy? Or, I can refer you to a colleague of mine, a physician on Harley Street who has particular skill in the care of the skin."

She responded by putting her left hand on the back of her neck and wincing quickly. "Oh, you must mean Dr. Lomaga. Thank you, Dr. Watson. It is just a minor skin affliction. Being of Irish descent, I inherited the complexion. It's nothing really, and I went to see Dr. Lomaga yesterday and gave me an ointment and told me that it would go away in a few days. Brought on by mental distress, he said. All I had to do was to relax, and my skin would clear. But I am afraid that there has not been a chance to do that. But perhaps I could if I knew that you and Sherlock Holmes were helping me find my mother."

"Which," said Holmes, "indeed, we are. You may relax your mind and body."

"Oh, thank you, Mr. Holmes. Thank you. You are too kind. Thank you. And please do not think badly of me if I now have to speak of how I might be able to pay you. You are far too decent a gentleman to bring up the matter but I assure you that I am not here is ask for charity. I have a bit saved from my time in Europe and could pay that as a deposit. And then as soon as I start to work again, I promise to send a bit of my salary every fortnight until everything has been paid. I am proud to say, Mr. Holmes, that I have never asked anyone for charity and never accepted any when offered. I will pay, sir, honestly, I will. You will just have to give me time."

She had opened her gorgeous green eyes wide and was gazing at Holmes like an affectionate puppy dog.

"My dear young lady," he said, smiling warmly. "Now is not the time to be worried about that matter. You keep your savings, my dear. You will need them to live on until you secure your next contract. Once you have found another lucrative arrangement, we can discuss the payment of my fee. I am not offering you charity, but until then, there will be no fee and no expenses charged. Is that acceptable to you?"

"Oh, Mr. Holmes, Mr. Holmes. You are an angel. I knew that you were a brilliant detective, but I could not have known that you were also such a kind Christian gentleman. Oh, thank you, sir. Thank you."

She was now beaming radiantly at my friend. The look was so warm that had there been frost on the window, it would have melted in an instant. The three of us continued for several more minutes with inconsequential chat, and then Miss Lightowlers rose to leave. Holmes immediately stood up and faced her.

"It has been a pleasure, Miss Lightowlers," he said, and then in a manner most uncharacteristic of him, he held out his left hand, palm facing up, just above her right hand. She responded in the appropriate manner and placed her hand in his. He raised it up and bowed forward to kiss it. The action exuded old-world manners and charm, and for that reason alone, Holmes had never done anything like it before. Mrs. Hudson returned to the room, bearing the young woman's coat and saw her to the door. I poured myself a generous snifter of brandy, leaned back in my chair and glared at Holmes. He was serenely looking off toward the bay window.

"Do you believe her, Holmes?" I demanded.

"What? Believe her? Not entirely. Some of what she said has most likely been fabricated. Such is standard practice when a new client is fearful and not yet fully trusting me. But she seems fundamentally truthful. Would you not agree?"

"Quite frankly, Holmes, no. Even I could see that she was far from being entirely forthcoming."

"You don't say. How so, Watson?"

I could not believe that Holmes had been such a dullard. "She claimed," I said sharply, "to have come by cab. She did nothing of the sort. She came by the Underground and must have walked from the Metropolitan Station. I could smell the residue of tobacco smoke from a crowded Underground car. And she said she was poor. Her dress and coat look as if she fetched them from a rag and bone shop, but surely you observed her boots?"

"Her boots, you say. Yes, what about them?"

"What about them? They were Church's. Beautiful bespoke. A pair of them must run at least fifty pounds. It is unthinkable that a secretary could ever afford such a pair."

"Oh, come, come, Watson. Good quality shoes are one of the wisest investments any woman, or man for that matter, can make. It is mere proof that she responsibly saved her income and then spent it very sensibly. A certain sign of her judgment and temperament."

"They did not strike me that way," I protested. "But what about her perfume. Surely you noticed that. It was one of the most select brands ..."

"*Mille fleurs*," interrupted Holmes. "Yes, wasn't it intoxicating?"

"Holmes, a bottle of that costs a month's wage. Three months for a working woman. I gave my wife a very small bottle for Christmas. It ran me over thirty pounds. How could she afford that?"

"My dear doctor, you have answered your own question."

"I beg your pardon."

"Did your good wife save up her pin money and buy the perfume herself? No. It was a gift from a man who adores her, one who has excellent taste and shows his affection by lavishing fine gifts upon her. Of course, I noticed it. Beyond a doubt, it was a gift from one of her many gentlemen admirers. She had the good sense and steel of soul to accept the gift and then send whoever it was packing. Quite the woman, would you not agree?"

No, I thought, I would not. But there was no use arguing with Holmes. All I could do was speak my mind to him.

"Holmes, I do believe that she has bewitched you."

"Oh, my dear chap," he said, with a smile and a low laugh, "of course I am attracted to her. I am not entirely that calculating machine you have accused me of being. If a beautiful young woman comes asking for my help in the depths of winter when interesting cases have ebbed for the season, why would I not be willing to help her? It would be so much more enjoyable than sitting in this stuffy room. Or would you rather I used my old solution to ease my boredom."

"No. Of course not."

I could say no more and picked up a medical journal that I had brought with me. Holmes turned his chair toward the bay window, lit up a cigarette, and gazed off serenely into the winter sky.

Chapter Two
Miss Gertrude Hume-Craw

When I finished reading the short article in the medical journal, I put it down and looked over at Holmes. I was somewhat relieved to see that his look of heavenly peace had vanished. Now his eyes were closed, his hands, with fingertips touching, were in front of his chin, and a small scowl creased his forehead.

"When," I asked, "do you expect your next appointment?"

"In four minutes," he replied, without opening his eyes.

In precisely that amount of time, a firm knock came to the door, and Mrs. Hudson descended the steps to welcome the visitor.

"Your next appointment has arrived, Mr. Holmes," she said after climbing back up to the room. "here is her card."

Holmes glanced at it quickly and handed it over to me. It was quite nicely printed and read:

Gertrude Hume-Craw

General Secretary
The Minoan Expedition
British Museum (Department of Antiquities)

"Mrs. Hudson," I said, with a sly grin on my face. "Are you not going to give Mr. Holmes a warning about this one?"

She smiled back at my tease. "Not unless he needs a scrum-half for his rugby team."

A minute later, Mr. Hudson reappeared, carrying what looked like to a military issue overcoat and followed by a rather imposing woman. Miss Gertrude was not underfed, but then again, not at all fat. The only word that I could use to describe her would be *powerful*. She was as tall as I am, as thick round the neck, and every bit as wide in the shoulders. Her hair was cut like a schoolboy's, and her face was devoid of any cosmetic enhancements. She took two quick steps into the room and barked at us.

"Which of you is Holmes?"

"I am Sherlock Holmes," said my friend. "Welcome, Miss…"

"So, you must be Watson," she interrupted, now looking at me.

"I am he."

"Good. I do not have much time to waste, so shall we begin?"

Without being asked, she strode over to the table, pulled out one of the straight-back chairs with one hand, spun it around, and sat down.

"How much do you charge for your services?" she demanded of Holmes.

"I do not usually…," began Holmes and got no further.

"Well, I usually do. So, let's get that over with."

Holmes looked a little nonplussed, but took a slip of paper and a pencil and wrote a number of it. He stretched out his long arm to hand it to Miss Gertrude.

"Sign it first," she said.

Holmes looked at her, and slowly his scowl changed into a bemused smile. He signed the note and handed it to her. She looked at it quickly.

"Right. I accept that," she said.

"There is," said Holmes, "a possibility that it might not apply to your case."

"Why not?"

"It only applies to cases I accept. And I have not yet accepted yours."

She shrugged. "You will. It's altogether too important and too intriguing for you to refuse, assuming that the tales Dr. Watson here writes about you are the truth. They are, aren't they?"

"Ah, yes. Sensationalised, romanticised, and with a regrettable paucity of attention to scientific deduction, but nevertheless true."

"That is what I thought. That is how I know you will accept my case."

"Very well, Miss," said Holmes, looking quite intrigued. "Kindly introduce your good self to us and state your case."

"I will. Are you familiar with my family name?" she asked.

"Yes," replied Holmes. "It is an uncommon portmanteau name, originally from the Borders and now applicable to several hundred families in Great Britain and several hundred more throughout the Empire. I must, however, assume that the question you meant to ask me was whether I know who your father is. And the answer to that is also affirmative. Professor Edgar Hume-Craw of St. Andrews University is a distinguished scholar of ancient history, an archeologist of some note, and currently the director of the Minoan Project, of which you are the General Secretary. Is that correct?"

She smiled a thin smug smile in return. "That is correct. Nice to see that you keep yourself informed."

"I am also informed," Holmes then continued, "that he is generally considered to play second fiddle to the far more renowned Arthur Evans, who has also been conducting archeological excavations in Crete on behalf of the Ashmolean Museum. Is that also correct?"

By the look on the woman's face, I was quite certain that had a paperweight or ink bottle been within her reach, she would have hurled it at Holmes. For a few brief seconds, she gripped the arms of her chair, stifling her anger. Then she replied.

"That is a matter of debate. Some consider Mr. Evans's success to be more the result of his political skills and the ability of his artist to restore ancient frescos so that they look as if they were painted yesterday than to anything approaching scholarship, but that is not what I came here to hire you for."

"I do hope not," replied Holmes, apparently enjoying the verbal jousting. "Why then did you come?"

"I came because my father is dead."

That was shocking news. Professor Hume-Craw was a figure of some reputation, and his death would surely have been reported in the Press.

"My condolences," I said. "We had no idea."

"Thank you, Dr. Watson. News of his death has not yet been released. Once it is, all of England will be aware of it. But I did not come here for your sympathy. I came primarily to hire Sherlock Holmes to investigate the death."

"You have my attention," said Holmes, "Now, give me the particulars, and I will tell you if I will take on your case."

She leaned back in her chair and folded her arms across her chest and began her account.

"I will not bore you with unnecessary historical details," she said. "You can do your own homework. I will tell you that after many years of scholarly research, my father had discerned the likely existence of an advanced civilization on the Isle of Crete that prospered for many years before the rise of the Athenian and Trojan empires. He, not Art Evans, named it the Minoan Era. For several years, using his private resources, he conducted preliminary diggings in Crete and finally, after months of delay, was awarded a substantial grant by the British Museum to carry out a large-scale archeological expedition. I am a very learned historical scholar in my own right, and I agreed to serve as the administrator of the expedition. By the time we arrived in Crete, Arthur Evans, by somewhat devious means, had already secured the site that my father had discovered, and we had no choice but to investigate what everyone considered to be a secondary site. As fate would have it, our site turned out to be to the location of a far greater treasure, of invaluable significance to the study of ancient history.

"Two weeks ago, we closed down our work for the season and boarded a boat that would bring us back to England by way of Athens, Palma, and Gibraltar. On the night we approached Gibraltar, there was a full moon, and the view from the deck was quite striking. My father got up from the table, saying that he was going outside to enjoy the vista. That was the last anyone saw of him. When we pulled into the port and disembarked for a brief time of re-stocking, all of us left the boat, but he did not appear. That was most uncharacteristic of him, and several of us went back on board to see if he was indisposed. We could not find him. We alerted the captain, and a full search was carried out. He was not on board. The captain concluded that he must have fallen overboard and agreed to request a full search of the waters approaching Gibraltar. The entire next day, the local officials, aided by a small fleet of fishermen, scoured the waters. He was nowhere to be found.

"The currents around Gibraltar, as I assume you know, are very powerful, and had he fallen into the sea and drowned, his body could have been swept away for miles. We agreed with the captain that the voyage must be resumed. The expedition's photographer remained in Gibraltar to continue the search, and the rest of us made our way to London, arriving back here just three days ago."

"Clearly," said Holmes, "you suspect foul play, else you would not be here."

"I do. My father had made many sea voyages, often in far heavier seas that we were traveling through. Also, for his age, he was in superb physical condition and could clamber up and down hills and mountains and excavation ladders with the best of them. Such a man does not just walk out onto the deck on a calm night and fall overboard."

"A most reasonable deduction," concurred Holmes. He said nothing for the next minute, and I could almost read the list of queries he was forming in his most unique brain. He gave me a nod as if to say that I should be ready to record the coming interrogation, and then turned to Miss Gertrude.

"Let us be thorough and begin at the start of the expedition. Were there any events that took place prior to your departure that might have given a reasonable person cause for alarm, or at least concern?"

"There were," the woman replied, "the usual inconveniences and delays during the weeks as we prepared to sail, but nothing out of the ordinary, except for one recurring issue."

"Yes, and what was that?"

"Mr. Holmes, how long does it usually take for a telegram to travel from London to St. Andrews?"

"It arrives within seconds. Under a minute," answered Holmes.

"Yes, it does. And it would be very peculiar, would it not, if the time stamped on the sender's copy of the form were a full fifteen minutes ahead of the time stamped on the receiver's?"

Holmes's eyebrows edged up ever so slightly. "Indeed, it would. And this happened more than once?"

"Yes, numerous times. No one noticed at first, as the receiver never sees the sender's copy. But as I was compiling the files and pinning the copies together before placing them in the records, the anomaly of one set of slips caught my eye. That caused me to examine other copies, and there were over twenty of them that had somehow been delayed. At first, I wrote it off to the sloppiness of the Royal Mail and their clerks, but that made no sense. The time stamps are now done mechanically by the postal station clocks. There was no reason for the delay."

Holmes again nodded. "That is of singular interest. Did the delays continue? Have you had time to check since you returned?"

"No, and yes. We received many telegrams whilst we were in Crete, mostly from the Museum. Immediately upon returning to London I went there straight away the first morning after the boat had docked to report my father's death and, giving the reason that I was responsible for the records of the expedition, asked for the copies of their telegram forms. They were supplied, and I examined them, but there had been no delays. Perhaps one or two minutes here and there, but that was normal for messages traveling all across Europe and through the underwater cable to the islands."

"Ah, that is significant," said Holmes. "Did you form the suspicion that someone had been intercepting your telegraph messages and delaying them, perhaps whilst making a copy before forwarding them to you?"

"You are the detective, Mr. Holmes, not me. You tell me."

Holmes nodded. "That I am and in good time, I shall. Ad was there any other cause for concern before leaving?"

"None."

"Any animosities during your time in Crete?"

"There were many hard feelings between our people and the Evans expedition, and I would never say for certain that they could not stoop to murder. But whatever animosity was expressed was entirely on our part toward them. The Evans people, whenever we encountered them, were quite civil although I am sure that they gloated mercilessly behind our backs."

"Quite understandable," said Holmes. "A common phenomenon amongst academic types. Very well, let us return to the boat on the night of your father's disappearance. How many passengers were there on board?"

"It was not a large ship. There was a total of only thirty people plus the crew. Our party consisted of seven. Almost all of the other passengers who initially boarded with us in Heraklion disembarked in Athens. The few who remained got off either in Palermo or Palma. Only one man continued all the way to London, and he was an elderly Orthodox priest. He was far too frail to have ever pushed my father overboard."

"Quite so," observed Holmes. "May I assume that you have concluded that the most likely suspects to have done harm to Professor Hume-Craw would be amongst the members of your own party?"

"Were you not listening to me? I repeat: you are the detective, not me. But I can see no reason why a Greek, Sicilian, or Spaniard, who had no idea who we were, would wish my father harm. It is possible that one of them was a hired killer. That vocation is not uncommon amongst those nationalities, but the finger would seem at first to point to one of our party. Yes."

"I assume that the expedition had acquired some valuable artifacts that were to be turned over to the Museum," said

Holmes. "The members of your party would have known about these objects, would they not?"

"Not entirely. There were some items that no one except my father knew the value of. And he alone kept the full detailed inventory, which we have not yet succeeded in finding."

Holmes paused his questions and lit a cigarette before continuing his cross-questioning.

"Your case," he said, "does indeed contain some singular aspects. So, pray tell; do you trust all of the members of your party?"

She gave Holmes quite the look of annoyance. "Of course not. Would you? Anytime there is a fortune to be had, or a scholarly laurel to be gained, greed and ambition take over. Surely you know that."

Holmes actually smiled at her. "I do indeed. Therefore, I suggest that you provide me with a list of the members of your party and whatever details you have concerning them."

"I thought you would never ask," came the reply, as she opened her satchel, withdrew a file, and handed it to Holmes.

"Excellent," said Holmes, as he, in turn, handed the file to me. "Now, you did say at the outset of our conversation, that the death of your father was your primary concern. By that, I would understand that there must also be a secondary concern. Would you kindly elucidate."

"My mother," she said.

"What about her?"

"She is the principal beneficiary of my father's estate, and there are significant funds, intellectual properties, and royalties that must be transferred to her."

"Do you need me to recommend a trusted solicitor?" asked Holmes.

"No, Mr. Holmes. I already have a solicitor. What I need is a detective."

"Pray tell."

"Because my mother has gone missing. We have not heard from her for the past several months. My inquiries concerning her have come back void. I would like for you to find her so that the matters of the estate can be concluded."

"That can be easily carried out," said Holmes. "Where was the last known address of Mrs. Hume-Craw?"

"I do not know."

"You do not know where your mother lived?"

"That is what I said, Mr. Holmes. My mother and father had been estranged for the past decade. My career kept me in contact with him, not her. They did not divorce, but she, perhaps out of spite, resumed the use of her maiden name."

"Such a practice is not unknown," said Holmes. "And what was her maiden name?"

"Golderton. Charlotte Golderton."

To Holmes's credit, not a flicker passed over his stone face. I had to bite my tongue to keep from sputtering out some expletive, but Holmes merely carried on.

"Duly noted," he said. "And what was your last known contact for Charlotte Golderton?"

"She kept a box at the E.C. post office. Beyond that, I have no idea. I have also been estranged from her for several years. However, I trust that with your contacts in the Royal Mail, you should be able to track her down."

The conversation did not continue long afterward. Miss Gertrude Hume-Craw soon rose, and herself summoned Mrs. Hudson to bring her coat. Then she departed, letting herself out.

"A coincidence, Holmes?" I asked, with a twinkle in my eye.

"Oh ho, Watson. I most certainly hope not. Cases that involve missing people, murder on the high seas, exotic artifacts, and clients who appear to be trying to hire and at the same time mislead me are so much more interesting. We really must find this Mrs. Golderton woman and discover what it is about her that has caused two women, who could not be more different from each other, both to claim her as their mother."

Holmes took out his pipe and slowly filled and lit it. Then he drew his long legs up under his body and took on his Buddha-like posture, his eyes closed. I opened the file that Miss Gertrude had left behind and perused the first page.

"Hell-o!" I involuntarily blurted. "What's this?"

"What?" said Holmes, not bothering to open his eyes.

"The members of the Minoan Expedition Party. You won't believe this one, Holmes."

"Then get on with it and tell me why."

I read off the names as they appeared on the first page.

"Expedition Director, Dr. Edgar Hume-Craw; General Secretary, Miss Gertrude Hume-Craw; Private Secretary to the Director, Miss Bernadette O'Donohue; Head of Excavations, Mr. Allister Baird; Head of Provisions, Mr. Robert Argyle; Head Curator, Mr. Darren Cruickshank; and ..." and here I paused, "Photographer ... Mr. Lloyd Sunday."

On hearing the last name, Holmes's eyes did pop open, and he rose from his chair and came over to look at the list.

"How singularly intriguing," he said. Without asking, he removed the file from my hands and took it back to his chair. He was soon oblivious to all but its contents.

I returned to my reading and, after enduring Holmes's silence for half an hour, interrupted him.

"Did you not say you had three appointments this afternoon? When is the next one due?"

He appeared startled and quickly glanced at his watch.

"Oh, thank you, Watson. I had put it out of my mind. The data already received this afternoon has rather consumed my attention. Now ... confound it. She is due any minute. Had you reminded me earlier, I could have sent a note putting her off for several days. Now we shall have to see her."

"A new client then?"

"Yes, another one of those poor, pathetic young women who claims that her employment situation is intolerable. No doubt some beast of a man, some masher demanding her affection. Please just take down her particulars, and I will try to get rid of her as quickly as possible.

Chapter Three
Miss Rowena Ferguson

T he bell soon sounded, and once again Mrs. Hudson answered the door and came back up the stair to report.

"Yes, Mrs. Hudson," said Holmes. "My dear, please do not just stand there. What is this one like?"

"Well, Mr. Holmes, I was about to say that she was the third young woman in the same afternoon, but I hesitated. The first visitor was no longer all that young, and the second was not exactly womanish. This one is both."

"Is she now? And no warning about her?"

"Very well, Mr. Holmes, it would be a very rapid judgement were I to make it, but I must say that if I had a son who was in need of a wife, I would arrange for him to meet Miss Rowena Ferguson before she was snapped up by a dozen other mothers of sons."

That, I thought, was about a generous an introduction as I had ever heard delivered by our dear landlady, and, over the years, she had introduced at least a hundred other women to Holmes in my presence.

"Ah," sighed Holmes, "a veritable priggish Sunday school teacher. Needy, but intolerably dull. Please show her up."

"I will, Mr. Holmes, and I will assure her that in her hour of need, Mr. Sherlock Holmes will give her his full and respectful attention."

She turned abruptly and went back down to the door. Holmes rolled his eyes and sighed.

"Very well, if I must, I must."

Mrs. Hudson soon returned with the young woman in tow and presented her to us. I had stood and glared at Holmes until he did likewise. As he would later admit, Mrs. Hudson's appraisal of this client was right on the mark. She was modestly dressed, bore no cosmetics on her face, kept her hair neatly up on her head and exuded the fragrance of mere soap and water. She was, nevertheless, uncommonly pretty. Had I been father to a son, I might well have agreed with Mrs. Hudson and paraphrased one much wiser than I in saying *behold, a Scot in whom there is no guile.*

"Please, Miss Ferguson, come in and be seated," said Holmes. "We are at the end of a long and busy afternoon, so kindly make yourself comfortable and state your case."

The young woman sat down and, keeping her back straight and her hands in her lap, spoke in a soft Scottish voice.

"Mr. Holmes, I am the victim of a vile blackmailer. As a result, I have stolen scores of valuable documents from my employer and passed them on to this man. Now, it appears that as a result of my actions, an important man may have been murdered." There she stopped and looked directly at Holmes, awaiting his response.

I could not recall any statement of a case being so concise and so quick to grab my friend's undivided attention. He put aside the file he had still been holding and looked intently at this most recent visitor.

"Thank you, Miss Ferguson. Forgive me if I seemed brusque. I assure you that you have my full attention. Could you kindly back up, fully introduce yourself and your situation and present the evidence that has led you to your conclusions?"

"Aye, sir, I can do that. I come from the town of Ayr in the south of Scotland. I am the only child of the Reverend Donald Ferguson, of the Church of Scotland and Mrs. Elizabeth Ferguson. I was raised in a godly home and my father, being a practical Scotsman, insisted that I learn some type of trade so that, should the good Lord not provide me with a husband, I would have an income of my own on which to live. I took up secretarial skills and excelled in my learning, so much so that I was advanced to the class of telegraph operator. I also performed well in those studies. A year ago, a notice came around saying that the Royal Mail was in need of telegraph operators in their large office in Mount Pleasant, which handles all of the mail and telegraphs coming and going from the EC. What with the war in the Cape and so many young men having been sent there, the Royal Mail had decided to hire women to replace them. Even if the wages were less than they had been paying the men, it was still an excellent billet and much beyond what I could ever hope to earn up in Scotland. My mother and father prayed about this opportunity and agreed that it was of such good fortune that it could not be turned down, and so I came to London, found my very own flat in Clerkenwell and began working.

"I did well in my duties and made many wonderful friends with the other young women with whom I was working. I attended some social functions with them and was introduced to a young soldier, a handsome Scottish laddie, Corporal Archibald MacDonald, with whom I fell quite hopelessly in love. For a month we spent every spare minute of our time together and then he was shipped out to the war. He had been gone for only a month when I realized that I was pregnant with his child. I immediately sent a telegram off to my beloved informing him and he, being an honorable man, replied immediately to say that he was thrilled and that we would be married as soon as he returned. I also took some steps that were deceitful, I must confess, but necessary, and went out and bought myself a simple wedding ring and told my employer that I had married a soldier the night before he was

34

sent off to war. The telegraph office is in great need of qualified operators, and I was one of the best, so they announced that they would not dismiss me but would praise me for my patriotic duty and allow me to keep working. They even allowed me to stay on after I began to show. It was out of a need for workers much more than for any enlightened ideal they might have held concerning the employment of women; nevertheless, it sufficed. I lived exceptionally frugally, saved every farthing I could, and then took three months off of my employment and delivered my son. Some of the girls I worked with, of course, knew my true situation but they breathed not a word to anyone. I deceived my parents and told them that what with the war, the demands at the Mount were so great that no one was allowed to take any holidays and so I could not return to visit them. They knew nothing and still know nothing about my situation.

"On the day I returned to my flat from the hospital, a telegram was waiting for me informing me that my fiancée had been killed in action in the Cape. I had leave of one week from my station, most of which I spent in tears, then I took my son to Bernardo's and asked them to find him a loving home. I knew I could not raise him on my own and I trusted them to find a loving Christian family. The next day I returned to my work."

As she spoke these last few sentences, I could hear the faltering of her voice. So must have Holmes for he interrupted her recitation and spoke to her in a kindly way.

"Miss Ferguson, permit me to be candid and forthright. If your parents are, as you say, loving Christian people, then surely they would forgive you and do everything in their power to support you and your child."

Tears appeared in the young woman's eyes. She took a deep breath and carried on.

"Mr. Holmes, I know what you say is right. But I simply could not bring myself to come to them as a fallen woman. Lying to them would just compound my shame. I am their only child and their pride and joy. It would break their hearts. My father is a minister in an austere denomination. Having a fallen daughter would be a cause for scandal in his congregation. I just could not bring myself to do that to them."

Holmes smiled in genuine warmth. "My dear young lady, there is a solution."

She looked up in wonder at Holmes. "What?"

"Arrange for a fortnight of leave from your station. Go to Bernardo's and reclaim your son. They do not send children out for adoption for several months if they arrive as infants. Then take your son and go home to your parents and congratulate them on becoming grandparents. The devastation they will feel at your having been overtaken in a fault will be canceled out by the irresistible joy of holding their grandson. You will face a short time of turmoil, after which your mother will make plans to spend every other week, if not more, in London, helping you care for her grandson. Your father will preach a sermon on the New Commandment Our Lord gave to his people or some other appropriate text, and if there is gossip within the congregation, your mother will remind them that, according to the scriptures, backbiters are to be sentenced to eternal damnation in the lake of fire and brimstone. I implore you to trust me on this advice. I have dealt with an abundance of grandparents in the past. Dr. Watson will wholeheartedly agree with me, will you not, Doctor."

"Entirely," I said. "Could not agree more."

Miss Rowena Ferguson was now trembling and struggled to reply.

"Mr. Holmes, I do not know how I could do that. I am not sure I have the strength to do what you ask."

"It is quite obvious, young lady, that you have more than sufficient strength of character to do what I am telling you, not asking you to do. And furthermore, if you do not agree this instant to do what I have told you to do then I shall refuse to even listen to any more of your case, and you may leave this place forthwith."

I was quite sure that Holmes, in his sincere interest in doing the best for this remarkable young woman, was bluffing. A case involving blackmail and murder was not something he would ever send packing. However, the young woman believed him. For a brief moment, she bowed her head and closed her eyes. Her moment of prayer was accompanied by a set of fiercely clenched fists.

"Very well, Mr. Holmes, I will do what you say. Now, may I please continue to state the rest of my case?"

"Yes, please do. You have my undivided attention."

"Thank you. It happened in this fashion. Several months into my pregnancy, I came to work and to my operator's desk, and I found, hidden under my key, an envelope. It was addressed to me, and the name and address were typed. The contents of the letter were also typed. The contents horrified me. Some vile creature had somehow become aware of many of the facts of my private situation, of my duplicity in lying about my marriage to my employer, and my fear of my family's shame because of me. The letter was very matter of fact, and the writer demanded that I either be willing to make copies of certain telegrams and send them to him, or he would inform my employer, my family and the Press of who I was and what I had done. I was sick with fear. For two days, I was frozen in inaction. Then another letter arrived, restating the demands and giving me just one more day to let him know my answer. I was instructed to write my reply and send it to an address in Belgravia, which turned out to be a private postal forwarding service.

"I was physically ill all that night, fearing that were I to stay in that state I would lose the baby I was carrying. So, early the following morning I wrote a letter to this evil man and agreed to his terms."

"Permit me to interrupt," said Holmes. "Was there no indication of who this man was? Any clue at all?"

"He signed his letters with a name, sir, if that is what you are asking."

"Precisely. And what was the name?"

"He signed as Mr. Charles Augustus Milverton."

Holmes was immediately silent and stared at her and then at me in disbelief. The young woman watched both of us and then she smiled.

"Oh, please, gentlemen. I knew it was a false name. Mr. Milverton's murder was reported in the Press some time back. He had been shot by two miscreants who had tried to rob him. I am sure you read that story, as did I. But I have no idea at all what his true name was."

"Thank you, Miss," said Holmes. "Pray, continue."

"I immediately began to receive instructions, coming again as notes that were waiting for me at my desk, explicitly directing me to make copies of telegrams by this noble lord, or that clergyman's wife, or some member of Parliament—all people of some social standing and wealth. I did as I was told, and sometimes I would receive more instructions immediately, and sometimes a week or two would pass without my hearing anything."

"Did anything," asked Holmes, "come of the data you intercepted and passed on? Was any action taken against the people whose secrets you had revealed?"

"With one exception, no. Nothing was ever heard about them. Which leads me to believe that they paid the demands made by the blackmailer."

"A logical deduction," noted Holmes. "And the one exception?"

"Do you recall the recent stories in *The Chronicle* about Bishop Worthington in the Cotswolds?"

The scandal the woman referred to had been in the Press the previous year. Several damning allegations were made concerning the austere bishop, his attraction to the love that dare not speak its name, and his clandestine meetings in the wooded copses of the Cotswolds.

"I do recall that unfortunate series of stories," said Holmes.

"I was the one," said the young woman, "who ruined that man's life."

"In fairness," said Holmes, "the cleric himself may have been solely responsible for his downfall. His punishment was well-deserved."

"What did," I interjected, "happen to that fellow? He just vanished."

"He was transferred to a rural diocese in Manitoba where the forests are either beyond frigid or infested with mosquitos. Any exposed flesh is immediately to mortal danger from one of the two. His parishioners are no longer in danger."

He turned back to Miss Ferguson.

"Pray, continue. You continued to obey the instructions?"

"Yes, and I lived in mortal fear that I would be found out and I was afraid that my fear would harm my baby. I had never been so terrified in my life.

"Then, one day as I was passing the desk of another one of the girls who worked alongside me, I noticed an envelope on her desk. It was addressed to Charles Milverton, at the same address that I sent my stolen information to. At first, I was dumbfounded, but then I realized that I was not the only one who Mr. Milverton had recruited to carry out his vile deeds. So, without saying anything to my colleague—Eleanor was her name—I casually sat down beside her during our tea break and whilst chatting about the weather, I slowly took an addressed enveloped from my purse and displayed it to her, all the while chatting away. The look on her face said it all. She said nothing and just pointed a trembling finger at me, and I silently mouthed back the words *me too* to her. Then, whilst still chatting about the weather, I wrote a note and slipped it to her. On it, I suggested that she meet me after work in the lady's lavatory in the nearest Underground station. We met there, quite sure that no one could overhear us and opened our hearts to each other. I told her about my family, and my son, and my lies to the Royal Mail, and the death of my beloved soldier. She replied in kind and informed me that Mr. Milverton had somehow discovered that she was married with two children, but that her husband was in prison for robbing a post office. Were it to be revealed, she would be terminated immediately. With her husband not able to provide any support, she was the only one who could look after the cost of food and clothing for her children and pay the rent. She knew that should she be forced to leave her employment, the three of them would be in the poorhouse within a week. She had received the same threats I had, and had also succumbed and had sent copies of many highly confidential telegrams to Mr. Milverton.

"I know it is hard to explain, but just knowing that there was one other human being in the same horrible situation as I was, gave me strength, as it did her. We began to meet briefly every day after our shift ended and we shared with each other what we had done that day.

"After a week of meeting, and becoming dear friends, Eleanor said to me that she thought there might be other girls in the same predicament. We came up with a plan to keep an eye on the Royal Mail post box on the pavement just outside the front door of the EC building. It did not take long until we recorded three other girls, making five of us, who were putting envelopes into the box regularly. We quietly approached each of them very privately, using the same actions as I had with Eleanor whereby we chatted about nothing while exposing an envelope with the address of Charles Milverton. Their reaction was the same as Eleanor's had been and we soon were able to set up clandestine meetings for the entire group of us. They alerted us to two more, making a total of seven. Every one of us had some secret that we could not dare to become known. One girl had shaken her baby so hard that it died in her arms. Another's mother worked every night over in Whitechapel as a prostitute. And another was involved in an illicit relationship with a bishop. All of our secrets had been discovered. We were each paying the price and had given in to blackmail.

"But, we were a spirited little team, if I say so myself. We came up with what we thought was a brilliant plan. We would continue to copy and forward all those highly confidential messages that were demanded of us, but we would alter the contents ever so slightly. Not enough to make it appear that we had rebelled, but enough so that the information if ever exposed, could be immediately proven to be false and slanderous, thus saving the reputation of the victim and making the data we were sending useless. We were quite proud of our bold counter-attack as we saw it."

"And did it work?" asked Holmes. "Were you able to implement your ingenious plan?"

"The four of us who continued to work in the Mount carried on for several weeks. Three of our number—Anna, Dorothy, and Bernie—quit their employment and sought greener pastures elsewhere that did not pay so well but that were free of such horrible demands. But then an odd thing happened, Mr. Holmes. We had been kept very busy with all sorts of demands, but then the notes suddenly stopped, for all of us."

"When was that?" asked Holmes.

"Just a bit over four months ago."

"You are quite certain of that?"

"Oh, very, sir. I could give you the exact date for I remember that the last demand I received was on my mother's birthday. The other remaining girls all said the same thing. It was as if a deadly weight had been lifted off our shoulders. We had no idea why the demands had ceased, but we were overjoyed."

"And may I assume," asked Holmes, "that your reason for coming to see me after such an extended period of freedom is because the demands started up again recently."

"Yes," she sighed. "That is exactly what happened. But, during our brief escape from our prison, I had read several dated copies of the Strand magazine in which the stories of your adventures were recounted. I made a pledge in my heart that should the horrid demands ever reappear, I would come immediately to Sherlock Holmes and place myself under your care. And that is why, sir, you find me here speaking to you this afternoon."

Holmes again smiled at her and replied. "I am honored by your confidence, Miss. So, shall we begin with first things first? You said that your actions might be related to a murder. Kindly explain."

"Yes, sir. I can do that, Mr. Holmes. Are you familiar with the name of Professor Edgar Hume-Craw?"

I came close to snapping in two the pencil with which I was taking notes. Holmes, as I expected, did not bat an eyelash.

"You refer to the learned historian from St. Andrew's. The Director of the British Museum's Minoan Expedition?"

"Yes, sir. That is who I mean. He died on his way back home from Crete. He fell overboard in the Mediterranean, and foul play is suspected. He and his expeditions were the subject of the demands for information immediately prior to the four-month lapse, and they were again over the past few days. I cannot prove anything, sir, but I am certain that he was murdered and that it was directly connected to all the data we sent to Mr. Milverton back in the fall."

Holmes nodded sagely and continued. "Was it indeed? Perhaps you could impart to me some of that data."

For the next ten minutes, Miss Ferguson recounted an extensive quantity of detailed information concerning the Minoan Expedition that had been shared by telegraph amongst the members of the party, and back and forth between its principals and the Museum. Her prodigious memory was most impressive and, when I later compared my notes to the information in the file that our previous visitor had left behind, I found that the details matched. I was familiar, from reading of the account of both this expedition and the more renowned one of Arthur Evans, with many of the place names in Crete and those of the various gods and temples. However, she quoted two archeological terms I had never heard of: *Linear A* and *Linear B*. It seemed that both of these were indecipherable ancient languages that had been discovered in Crete. Arthur Evans had claimed the credit for their discovery, but our now departed professor had claimed that he had solved the riddle and could translate them. Such an accomplishment would bring lasting fame and adulation to him and the party.

When she had completed her summary, Holmes then moved to the next stage in the case.

"Excellent, Miss Ferguson," he said. "now, about the telegraphs you perused in the past few days. What all did they speak of?"

"Mostly about the death of the professor. The chaps at the Museum were very distressed by the news, and they kept on asking about 'the priceless treasure' the professor was bringing to them. And there were also several references to two people that the members of the party and the officers of the Museum were very exercised to locate. They had somehow gone missing."

"And who," asked Holmes, "might they have been?"

"Their names were Charlotte Golderton and Lloyd Sunday."

We chatted on for some time before Miss Rowena took her leave. Holmes admonished her to continue in her subterfuge and counter-attack and not breathe a word to anyone about her visit to 221B Baker Street. And, of course, he reminded her of her promise to go as soon as possible back to her parents and disclose to them the entirety of her situation.

"I do believe, Watson," he said after she had departed, "that we have had a singularly intriguing criminal conspiracy dropped into our laps this afternoon."

"It would appear so."

"The intercepting of confidential telegraph messages by an unscrupulous blackmailer offers countless opportunities for crimes that will never be reported to the police. Would you agree?"

Chapter Four

The British Museum

During the following few days, I saw little of Holmes. He departed 221B early in the morning and returned after I had retired for the night. I knew he would be hot on the trail of Lloyd Sunday and the elusive Charlotte Golderton. When he did appear at the breakfast table on the Thursday morning, I began the conversation with the invariable question that every passerby makes to a man standing on a bridge who is holding a fishing rod.

"Any luck?"

Holmes shook his head and gave the equally invariable reply. "Not yet."

After a sip of his morning coffee, he added, "I have picked up the trail of the Lloyd Sunday chap. He returned to London from Gibraltar and has been moving to a new hotel every night. He clearly does not want to be found. But I expect to be able to track him down by the time he wakes up on Saturday morning."

"And Mrs. Charlotte? What about her?" I asked.

"Nothing. Nothing at all. No hotel registrations; no postal address, no news from my agents or Irregulars. Whoever she is, she has managed quite brilliantly to elude me."

"Even after your burning the midnight oil for four days straight," I said.

"Oh no. It has not been quite that bad, Watson. I only worked through two of the evenings. I spent the other two at the opera and the symphony."

I must admit that this admission left me speechless. Sherlock Holmes and I had been the closest of friends for over twenty years, and we always invited the other to join if we had plans to go to some entertaining event for the evening. My wife and I invariably sent a note asking him along. Usually, he declined, but sending the invitation was simply an unspoken rule of our friendship. I was not only surprised but, quite frankly, my feelings were hurt.

Holmes must have read the expression on my face and smiled at me warmly.

"My dear friend," he said. "Of course, I would have asked you to join me, but it was not I who arranged for the tickets. I was invited as a guest of Miss Lightowlers."

"The redhead? You spent the evening with *her*?"

"Yes, and dinner as well. Both occasions were quite pleasant. She is rather delightful company."

He said no more, and instead picked up the newspaper and began to read it whilst finishing his coffee. I was stunned. In all the years I had known him, he had never done anything like that. He had, I remembered, falsely pretended to court and even propose marriage to the maid at Appledore Towers, but that was no more than a ruse to gain entry to the home of Mr. Milverton. That he would spend an evening with a beautiful woman who was twenty years his junior, was unheard of. I was about to demand an explanation when he looked up over the newspaper and turned the conversation to something utterly unrelated.

"Could you spare me a couple of hours of your time this morning?"

"I suppose so," I replied. "My first appointment is not scheduled until eleven o'clock. What did you have in mind?"

"Splendid. Then please finish your coffee, don your coat, and join me for a visit to the British Museum."

The mysterious disappearance and presumed death of Professor Hume-Craw had become known and was now fodder for the Press. Newsboys across the north end of London were shouting about it all the way from Baker Street to Bloomsbury. Although there was not a shred of evidence as to who might have disposed of the professor and tossed him into the sea, it did not stop the press from speculating on the

Greeks, the Italians, or especially the Cretans. The divinely inspired words of St. Paul, informing Timothy that *all Cretans are liars* was cited as sufficient proof of the culpability of the descendants of the Minoans, regardless of the vast miles of sea that separated them from the Straits of Gibraltar.

The Museum, in Bloomsbury, is not that far from Baker Street and we had soon passed my *alma mater*, the University College of London, and were approaching the great square block in which the complex was located.

"Who are we meeting here?" I asked. "I rather doubt you are bringing me just to gaze one more time at Lord Elgin's trophies or the Portland Vase."

He smiled and replied, "We have an interview with Mr. Edward Thompson, the Director and Principal Librarian, and Fred Kenyon, the Director of Antiquities. I informed them yesterday that I was investigating the death of Professor Hume-Craw and received a reply back at once saying that they wished to meet with me at my earliest convenience."

As we pulled up to the main gate of the Museum on Great Russell Street, Holmes suddenly stuck his head out the window and instructed the driver to continue to the corner, then turn left and proceed once more around the block before returning to the gate to let us out.

"Forgive my being nostalgic, Watson," he said as we turned onto Montague Street. "Just up ahead on the right is the house that I first lived in before we met each other. I could only afford a small single room but it was my first home in

50

London, and I have some pleasant memories of it and the neighborhood."

I did not bother to look at the house as we passed it. Instead, I sat and looked at Holmes, wondering what had come over him. In all the years I had known him, he had not once wallowed in pleasant memories of the past. Nor had he voluntarily spent an evening with a single woman. Suddenly, a side of his character was on display that he had kept hidden very well for a very long time.

As we completed our run around the circumference of the Museum block, Holmes sat with his eyes closed and a serene smile on his face. I was relieved when the cab finished its circumnavigation and stopped again at the gate. This time we got out and walked through the gate, past the rows of Ionic columns, and into the far reaches of the museum.

"Mr. Sherlock Holmes and Dr. Watson. Good of you to come on such short notice."

The well-dressed gentleman who stood stiffly at the door of a small conference room on the top floor welcomed us. We were ushered to chairs at an elegant table in an ornate room. On the walls and in small alcoves were numerous pieces that I assumed were priceless treasures of art that the Empire had purchased, bartered for, and outright stolen and smuggled from the four corners of the earth.

"Permit me to introduce myself," said the fellow who had greeted us. "I am Dr. Frederick Kenyon, the Director of the

Antiquities Department. Please, be seated, and I will let Dr. Thompson know that you have arrived."

He departed and returned a few moments later with another finely attired but considerably older gentleman.

"Dr. Watson and Mr. Holmes," said Kenyon, "allow me to introduce Dr. Edward Thompson, our esteemed overall head of the Museum."

The older man smiled congenially and sat down.

"Gentlemen," he began, "I normally begin any meeting held in this room with a few boastful paragraphs about the largest and finest museum in the world. I will dispense with my customary braggadocio and get straight to the purpose of our meeting. I have been given to understand, Mr. Holmes, that you have been contacted by Miss Gertrude Hume-Craw and contracted to investigate the death of her father."

"Yes," said Holmes. "I have."

"Brilliant. Then kindly report to us on what you have discovered to date."

Holmes gave the old boy a cool stare.

"I was not aware that the British Museum had contracted for my services."

"Dash it all, Mr. Holmes," said Thompson, "Miss Hume-Craw is our employee, and it was our expedition. We paid for it. If you are worried about collecting your fee, let me assure you that this Museum has more money than God and is prepared to cover any and all of your costs. What we need is information, and we need it now." He banged his walking stick on the floor for emphasis.

"If you say so," acknowledged Holmes. "I appreciate your strong concern over the loss of one of your expedition's leaders."

That comment brought the walking stick down on the floor one more time.

"Good Lord. We are not here to bemoan the fact that Hume-Craw fell overboard. He was probably drunk, or one of his Greek peons gave him the heave-ho. It matters not. We have an entire long shelf full of reports of expeditions that lost a member, or a director, or an entire expedition. Every other year some damned fool sails off again to find John Franklin. We have expeditions that got lost looking for lost expeditions, and then a few more who got lost looking for those ones. No, Mr. Holmes. We are quite used to losing men in the pursuit of discovery. And why? Look up there, Mr. Holmes."

He pointed to the top of the far wall. An inscription in Latin read: *Dulce et Decorum Est Pro Scientia Mori.*

"You do remember your Latin, do you not, Mr. Holmes?"

"As a detective, I am accustomed to repeating '*cui bono?*' several times a day," said Holmes.

"Ah, well put," the old fellow said, again with a solid tap on the floor. "Who benefits, you ask? All of mankind. We exist here for the pursuit of knowledge, for the discovery of previously unknown facts, for lifting the scales from the eyes of mankind, and for the revealing of truth. It is the truth that makes you free. The entire earth is the beneficiary of our expeditions."

"And this museum benefits as well, no doubt," added Holmes.

"Bloody right, we do. And we do not flinch from admitting it. You are sitting in the leading museum of the British Empire, and blast it, we are not going to be bested by the French, or the Russians, and certainly not by the Americans."

"Or," added Holmes, "by the Ashmolean?"

"Those upstarts? No, especially not by them. They had the good luck to have that Evans fellow as one of their former directors, and now they have been beating the pants off of us in unearthing the wonders of the ancient world. Hume-Craw's find would have put paid to that nonsense."

"I fear I do not understand," said Holmes. "What precisely was it that he discovered that you are so concerned to have brought here?"

Dr. Thompson looked over at the Director of Antiquities and nodded. "Dr. Kenyon, if you would, please."

The younger man rose and from a bookshelf retrieved four large volumes. These he placed on the table as the four corners of a square that was about a yard along each side. Then, from another shelf, he brought a long cardboard tube. From it he extracted a roll of paper and then spread it out on the table, anchoring the four corners of it with the books.

"Gentlemen," said Dr. Kenyon. "Please, come a take a close look. This is what Professor Hume-Craw discovered. The drawing was prepared by the expedition's photographer. The professor insisted that it was quite an accurate representation on a one-to-one scale. The actual piece is made of solid gold and in pristine condition."

Holmes and I rose and walked around to the other side of the table and took a close look. Suddenly, I felt an unexpected and uncontrolled blush coming to my face.

"Do you remember the story that it represents?" asked Dr. Kenyon.

"How could I forget?" replied Holmes. "It was every schoolboy's favorite. We giggled about it in the refectory for days on end. There was a contest amongst us to see who could find the most detailed and explicit account of it in the library."

The picture was of a small statue. The base was about a foot square, and two inches thick. The two figures on top of the base rose another foot. One was of a large bull, standing on his hind legs. The other was a beast that had the back end of a cow and the front of the face and naked torso of a female human. They were copulating.

"Yes. Isn't it exquisite," said Dr. Kenyon as he looked upon the drawing, his face aglow. "The ancient story of Poseidon's bull, so beautiful a bull that Parsiphaë fell in love with him. She had Daedalus construct a wooden cow that she climbed inside so that she could consummate her love."

"If I remember correctly," I said. "That story did not end well. Wasn't there a Minotaur that came along nine months later."

"Ah, yes. What an exciting story, is it not?" said Dr. Kenyon. "So beautifully depicted by an ancient craftsman whose name we shall never know."

"You say," said Holmes, "that this statue is made of solid gold."

"Yes," snapped Dr. Thompson, again with a tap on the stick. "But that is not why we want it here so urgently. This museum is overflowing with carved gold. A few more pounds, even a hundredweight, would not make much difference. What we want it for is what is written on the base. You cannot see that in the drawing."

On the drawing, there were a series of lines with squiggles and random scratches. They were meaningless.

"What do you know," demanded Dr. Thompson, "of what that Arthur Evans rascal has brought back to the Ashmolean?"

By now, I had read several accounts of the Evans expedition to Crete. He had uncovered the great temple of Knossos near Heraklion. Underneath the temple was a maze of walls that Evans had claimed was the ancient Minoan structure in which the Minotaur had been imprisoned. He had named the intricate cellar The Labyrinth. On the site, he had discovered several hundred clay tablets on which were the two distinct sets of markings that Miss Gertrude Hume-Craw had spoken of.

"He brought," I said, "all those clay tablets. But nobody knows how to read them."

"Exactly," said Dr. Kenyon. "He named the two languages Linear A and Linear B. They appear to be one of the first written phonetic languages known to man. Professor Hume-Craw wrote to us to say that one side of the base of this lovely work of art is a record of the story of Parsiphaë, written in Linear A. One another side is the same story, written in Linear B."

"If those languages," said Holmes, "are undeciphered, how can he say for sure what story it is they tell?"

"An excellent question, Mr. Holmes," said Dr. Kenyon. "The answer, unknown beyond a very few scholars, and will now be expanded to include you, is that the third and fourth sides contain the same story, but written in the oldest version known of ancient Greek. It is a veritable Rosetta Stone of the earliest civilization to have occupied the Mediterranean. It is a priceless find. It opens the door to an entire world of knowledge. And it is the property of the British Museum."

"And may I presume," said Holmes, "that once it arrived here, all the world shall have to bring their clay tablets and statues that contain those two Linear languages if they want to have them translated?"

"More or less," said Dr. Kenyon, smiling. "Of course, we shall eventually publish a dictionary of sorts in which the codes will be revealed. Perhaps we shall do that some twenty years from now. But until then, this museum shall be the center of the entire globe for the scholarly study of the earliest days of Western Civilization."

"And your primary wish," queried Holmes, "is for me to find this statue and get it back to you as soon as possible. Your interest in finding out who murdered your expedition's director is secondary. Is that correct?"

"Precisely, Mr. Holmes. Of course, we all wish to see nasty culprits brought to justice. But that concern falls under the aegis of the fellows in Foreign Affairs and Scotland Yard. We are scholars, sir, not policemen."

"Understandable," said Holmes. "Will you permit me to ask a few more questions before agreeing to take on this case?"

"Go ahead," said the older fellow. "But make it snappy. I do not have all day."

"Nor do I," said Holmes. "Kindly confirm to me the names of the members of the expedition. From the work I have conducted so far, I was informed that in addition to the Director, the members were: Miss Gertrude Hume-Craw, General Secretary; Miss Bernadette O'Donohue, Private Secretary to the Director; Mr. Allister Baird, Head of Excavations; Mr. Robert Argyle, Head of Provisions; Mr. Darren Cruickshank, Head Curator; and Mr. Lloyd Sunday, Photographer. Were there any others?"

"No," answered Dr. Thompson.

"Are you prepared to vouch for the scrupulous probity of the members of the expedition?"

"Those who are known to us, yes," replied Thompson. "We cannot speak for the others."

"And who amongst them is which?" asked Holmes.

"Miss Gertrude is a respected member of the staff of the Museum. The three young men are all from St. Andrews University and came with excellent letters of recommendation from their professors. Miss O'Donohue we only met briefly, and her background and her people are unknown to us, but we have no reason to have less than full confidence in her."

He stopped there.

"And Mr. Sunday?" pressed Holmes. "You did not mention his name."

"Ah, yes, that fellow, the photographer," said Thompson.

"Indeed," said Holmes. "What of him?"

"He has accompanied Professor Hume-Craw on several previous expeditions, and he takes excellent photographs. He and the professor were not fond of each other, but Edgar kept hiring him all the same. That is all I can say about him," said Thompson.

"That is instructive," said Holmes and then gave both of the museum men a hard look.

"Are you aware," continued Holmes, "of any illicit liaisons between members of the expedition? If so, between whom?"

"I beg your pardon!" said Dr. Kenyon. "That is hardly a question that is asked of gentlemen."

"It is," said Holmes, "a question that is asked by a detective. And I shall add to it a corollary. Were either of you or any officers or directors of the museum carrying on an illicit liaison with any members of the expedition?"

"That is enough, Mr. Holmes," came Kenyon's loud response. "If this is how you conduct your investigation, you can get out of the British Museum this instant and never come back."

Holmes merely smiled and turned to face the older fellow.

"Am I to leave, Dr. Thompson?"

The old man smiled back at him. "It appears that it is not without reason that Sherlock Holmes has become England's most famous detective. I have been on this earth long enough to know that *cherchez la femme* is an efficient place to being almost any investigation into matters of illegality. You may continue, Mr. Holmes."

"Very well, then kindly answer my question."

"Mr. Holmes," said Dr. Thompson, "I am seventy-five years of age. I fear that even if I wished to have done so, such a liaison would remain a chimera. I can also vouch for Dr. Kenyon. Even though he is a vigorous man in the prime of life, he is a married man and a faithful member of the Church of England. His reputation is beyond reproach."

"And amongst the members of the expedition? What of them?"

"They are all scholars," said Kenyon. "I would never stoop to indulging in the spreading of rumors behind their backs."

"And you, Dr. Thompson?" asked Holmes.

"Would I stoop to idle gossip, of course not? Would I believe something that appeared to be quite obvious? Unfortunately, yes."

Poor Dr. Kenyon stared at his superior and looked aghast. "Really, sir."

"I am afraid so." Then turning to Holmes, the old fellow continued. "Edgar Hume-Craw and his wife have been estranged for many years. It was well-known if not openly spoken of, that he was a bit of a bounder when it came to hiring attractive younger women to serve as his assistants. He cared as much for their amorous inclinations as he did for their ability to keep books and write letters."

Holmes now turned to Dr. Kenyon. "Please answer frankly, sir. Are you of the same opinion?"

"Mr. Holmes," protested Kenyon. "There were no reports whatsoever of anything like that taking place on the Minoan Expedition. Furthermore, I govern my tongue by *de mortuis nil nisi bonum.*"

"I am not asking about what he is doing now that he is dead. Only what he did whilst living. Please answer frankly."

The chap looked very uncomfortable but raised his head and spoke to the far window.

"If you insist, sir. Although I had no proof whatsoever, I assumed that the Director had a romantic interest in the secretary he hired, Miss O'Donohue. I only met her once, but she was highly attractive."

"And might there have been any other liaisons taking place?" asked Holmes.

"The only other female member of the expedition," replied Kenyon, "was the professor's daughter, Miss Gertrude Hume-Craw. I do not wish to speak unkindly, but suffice it to say that she did not strike me as the type of woman that men would be eager to engage."

"Thank you, sir," said Holmes. "Very well then, with regards to this missing statue, why did the photographer not take a photograph of it? Why make such a complete drawing?"

"Ah, that question," replied Kenyon, "affords an easy answer. They were in Crete, sir. There were no facilities available for the processing of the plates from the camera. All those had to be transported back to England before the photographs could be developed. Therefore, the sketch was drawn instead and sent back through the post."

"Thank you," said Holmes. "A most reasonable thing to do. Now, one final point of inquiry, if I may. What is the connection of Miss, or perhaps Mrs. Charlotte Golderton to this expedition?"

"You mean Madame Charlotte Europa Golderton?" asked Kenyon.

"If that is her full name, then yes. Was she a member of the expedition? Who is she? And where is she?"

"Might I ask, Mr. Holmes, how it is that you know this name?"

"Your telegraph messages back and forth with the expedition were intercepted, copied, and made known to me."

"That is quite alarming, Mr. Holmes," said Kenyon.

"That matter we can address at a later date. Today, I am asking you to tell me about this woman, Miss or Mrs. Golderton."

"Mr. Holmes, she is no one alive today and is nowhere," said Kenyon, smiling smugly. "Charlotte Europa Golderton is the name that Hume-Craw made up and gave to the woman portrayed in the statue."

"I regret that I do not understand," said Holmes

"In the earlier Minoan version of the story," said Kenyon, "it was Europa, the mother of King Minos who engaged with Zeus, in the form of the bull. The bowdlerized version records that he changed back into human form before violating her. The original account does not. A later version of the myth changed the participants to Poseidon's bull and Parsiphaë, who became the unfortunate mother of the Minotaur. It is quite common for antiquarians to give pet names to some of the statues they discover. The professor dubbed this magnificent statue, Charlotte Europa Golderton. Where he came up with the Christian and surnames, I have no idea. We here, on learning that the statue also had Greek wording inscribed on its base, judged it to be of somewhat later origin and so assumed that it was depicting Parsiphaë. We used the name concocted by Professor Hume-Craw when sending telegrams back and forth so as to conceal the matter being inquired after. I am sorry to disappoint you on that score, Mr. Holmes, but no flesh and blood Miss Charlotte exists."

Not long after this exchange, Holmes and I stood on the pavement of Great Russell Street. I continued to scribble notes from our meeting while he stood still, smoking a cigarette.

"I thank you, Watson, for your time this morning. I trust I have not caused you to keep your patients waiting."

"It would not be the first time, nor will it be the last that a doctor keeps people waiting," I replied. "But before I leave, I should like to know what you thought of our meeting. You have not one but two clients who lied to you about looking for their mother when what they wanted from you was to find a missing statue named Charlotte."

"And an exceptionally valuable one at that," said Holmes. "Well worth hiring my services for, would you not agree?"

"Holmes," I protested. "They lied to you."

"I might have done the same were I in their place. The last thing they want known by the Press is that this priceless treasure has gone missing. Quite clever to pretend that it is a missing person."

I was more than somewhat exasperated with him. "I will take a cab now, and shall I see you at supper?"

"No. I shall be otherwise engaged."

"With Miss Lightowlers? Again?"

"Yes, my dear Watson. Again."

He gave me a warm smile and a clap on the shoulder. Then turned and walked towards the Tottenham Court Road station of the Underground. For a full minute, I watched him, all the while shaking my head in disbelief.

Chapter Five
St. Andrews, Scotland

That evening, Holmes did not return to 221B until well after midnight. The following morning, he shuffled out of his bedroom as I was preparing to depart for my surgery.

"Good morning, Holmes," I said. "And did you have a pleasant evening? What was it this time? Dinner at Simpson's and then the opera? Or the theatre?"

"Oh, no neither," he replied, yawning. "We had some delightful fish and chips and then a rollicking evening at the music hall."

I was stunned. "Did you say *the music hall?*"

"I did indeed."

"Holmes, you despise the music halls. Every one of them. Have you lost your mind?"

"*Au contraire, mon ami.* I prefer to think that I have discovered my soul. I laughed heartily all evening, as did the quite enchanting lady who accompanied me."

I bit my tongue to avoid some unkind exclamatory response, and quickly grabbed my coat and smartly descended the stairs. I pulled the door behind me, perhaps a little more forcefully than was necessary.

Partway through the morning, a note was delivered to my medical office. It ran:

```
Watson: Could you be so kind as to cancel
any appointments you might have over the
weekend and join me on a journey to St.
Andrews? We will meet with some other
members of the Hume-Craw Expedition. Shall
return by late Sunday night. Meet tomorrow
morning at Flying Scotsman platform at
Kings Cross. 7:00 am.  Holmes
```

I was greatly relieved. I had convinced myself that Holmes would spend the entire weekend mooning over the admittedly attractive Miss Lightowlers and neglect his pursuit of what was emerging as a most unusual case. Now it appeared that his common sense had returned.

I did not see Holmes at all that evening, nor early the following morning, and I feared the unspeakable worst. But as

I entered the platform at King's Cross, I saw him waiting for me. At the far end, adjacent to the first-class cabins, was the tall, slender figure that had become so much a part of my life for the past twenty years. He was waiving at me merrily and smiled as we clambered into our cabin.

"So good of you, Watson, to join me. The game is afoot, and I do not know what I would do without my Boswell to keep track of it."

"Always a pleasure to do my part," I replied.

"I apologize," he said, "in advance for my about to become a dull traveling companion. Our enjoyable conversation will have to be brief. I have an entire valise of reading material to consume before we get to Edinburgh."

"On one condition," said I.

"Oh, and what, my friend, is that?"

"As your friend, who cares for you very deeply, I demand to know what your intentions are concerning Miss Ruth Lightowlers?"

He looked surprised at my question. "Good heavens, Watson. Why do you concern yourself about that? You must admit that you have had a far greater attraction to the fairer sex that I ever have. I am merely catching up to you." He smiled and brought a friendly fist down on my knee.

"*You* must admit that your sudden interest is highly uncharacteristic of your entire life to date."

"I admit that I have deprived myself of what is regarded by sensible men the world over as one of life's truly great pleasures—the company of a beautiful, intelligent, charming, and witty woman. And to top it off, she seems to find me similarly attractive. It must be my tall, lean figure. Who is to say?"

"Holmes, she is more than twenty years younger than you are."

"My dear Watson, your lovely wife, Mary, is a decade younger than you. What is a few more years? And besides, she has no interest in breeding a litter of little Sherlocks, and I have no intention of siring any. So, what is the issue if there is to be no issue?"

He chuckled at his witticism. I was beyond words and could only sputter, "But Holmes ..."

He lifted his hand, palm facing me. "Enough, my kind friend. I have far too much work to do, and I am sure that you can consume yourself with writing for several hours."

He then extracted several bound notebooks from his valise. Two bore the imprint of the Ashmolean Museum, and three the mark of the British Museum.

"By the time we reach St. Andrews," he muttered, "I shall be a minor expert on the Minoan Civilization of ancient Crete."

For the next eight hours, the train sped its way north to Scotland. I had not returned to the land of my birth since taking the high road to England so many years ago and had neither close kith or kin still living here. My view from the train window of my home country and city convinced me that it had changed not at all and most likely would not do so in the near future.

Holmes said nothing as we changed trains at the grand Waverly Station and quickly found the local train up to St. Andrews. It was approaching the supper hour when we checked into the old Rusacks Hotel. During the season, it is a favorite of golfers from around the globe as they come to claim boasting rights for having played The Old Course and genuflected at the eighteenth hole.

"This hotel," said Holmes, "has a fine restaurant, if any establishment that still serves mutton and haggis can ever be described that way. I am told that the finnan haddie is an excellent choice to begin a meal, and the poached salmon and shoulder of lamb are both quite delectable. The three young scholars who were part of Hume-Craw's expedition are joining us for dinner. I expect that they will be very pleased with the short but enjoyable departure from the food they are accustomed to in the university refectory."

Waiting for us at the entrance to the dining room were Messrs. Baird, Argyle, and Cruickshank. They were well-dressed for a dinner meeting although two of the suit jackets subtly announced *borrowed-and-a-size-too-large*.

Nevertheless, they were all fine specimens of young manhood—handsome, average to tall in height, and fit. We introduced ourselves to each other and were seated at a table by the window, affording us an excellent view of the North Sea and the Old Course. After enjoying a few mandatory minutes of idle chat, Holmes reminded the fellows of the purpose of the meeting.

"Would each of you," asked Holmes, "please explain to me the roles and responsibilities you had on the expedition."

They did as requested in a succinct manner. Obviously, they had expected the question and had rehearsed their answers so that they might make a good impression on the most famous detective in Great Britain. While they affected a refined Edinburgh accent, there was no mistaking that their counties of origin lay closer to Glasgow. Their speech betrayed them.

Holmes subsequently asked them to give, in the greatest detail they could muster, an account of the evening when their ship pulled into Gibraltar and the professor disappeared.

"Auch," began Cruickshank, the redhead of the lot. "it haed been a lovely evenin'. We waur sittin' at the table an' chattin.' Then the professor got up and says he's goin' for a wee stroll along the deck. Nobody thought anythin' of it, as the auld fellow liked his walks. An' wasnae'at the lest we saw of him."

"Did the rest of you remain at the table?" asked Holmes.

"Aye, we did, but only fur puckle fare minutes. Then we all departed."

"And where did you go?"

"I can only speak for myself and my two colleagues here. We all went back to Allister's room and played a few rounds of cards. We had become guid friends after four months of trial and tribulation together. It wasna 'til mornin' that any of us knew that the auld bloke haed disappeared."

71

"And the other members of your party? Did you see where they went?"

"Lloyd went off in the direction of the bar, as he aye did. Didna see where the ladies went."

"Did they depart together?" asked Holmes. "Most women do keep other company after men depart from the table."

"Those tois? Nae on your life. Unless it was tae stand at fife paces and fling knives at each other."

The other two young fellows nodded, and Holmes immediately demanded an explanation.

"Auch, sir. There was nae loove lost atween them, sir."

"And why was that?"

The fellow suddenly appeared hesitant to respond. He glanced over at his friends, and the Baird chap answered.

"You know how it is with the Scots and Irish, Mr. Holmes."

Holmes gave the young man a hard look.

"I know how it is when a man does not speak the truth. Scottish and Irish women have gotten along quite well for years even if their men have been at odds. Now, sir, please answer my question."

"Very well, sir," said Cruickshank. He continued slowly and deliberately, his accent all but gone.

"We do not wish to tell tales out of school, sir. But if you insist, I shall try to be candid. Miss Gertrude, as you know, sir, is Professor Hume-Craw's daughter."

"I am aware of that. Carry on."

"And Miss O'Donohue was his personal secretary, who had been hired only for the expedition. Being gentlemen scholars, we never spoke of it … well, perhaps not more than once, maybe twice … but we all knew that the friendship between the professor and Miss O'Donohue was quite intimate. It is understandable that a daughter might take exception to another woman who is the same age or younger than her sharing her father's bed. And so, the two of them were more than a little frozen in the way they got along."

"Thank you," said Holmes. "Very well, no more on that matter. So, if the ladies did not spend time together, where did each of them go?"

"Well sir, Miss O'Donohue says she would go and chat with the professor and see if he needs anything. And Miss Gertrude made a rather unkind remark in reply."

"Yes. What did she say?"

"She said, sir, something along the line of 'we'll be at the dock in a few hours. I am sure he can find a brothel there.' Or something close to that. Wouldn't you say?" He directed the last question to his friends, who nodded in agreement."

"Ah," said Holmes, "so this Miss O'Donohue was the last person to see the professor alive. Is that correct?"

"Nae. Lloyd, Mr. Sunday that is, told the police that at close to midnight, the professor came into the bar and had a wee dram, bade him good night, and went off. That's what he said."

Holmes asked several more questions, but the three men could offer no new information about the final hours of Professor Hume-Craw. Thus, he turned to another subject.

"I have been told that a priceless treasure was discovered at the temple you were excavating. Would you describe it to me?"

His question was followed by an awkward silence before Mr. Cruickshank replied.

"Aye. We were told that as well, Mr. Holmes. But it was found by one of the diggers late in the evening, and he brought it straight to Dr. Hume-Craw. The doctor cleaned it up by himself and had Lloyd Sunday take a picture of it, before putting it in his safe in his cabin. We never saw it, sir, only the sketch done by Lloyd."

Holmes looked at the other two, and they nodded their agreement. "Nae, sir. We never saw it. That's right," said Baird.

"And what about his secretary, Miss O'Donohue? Did she see the actual artifact?"

"You would have thought she did," said Cruickshank, "seein' as it came late to his cabin. But she was there when Lloyd rolled out his drawing, and she was as amazed as the rest of us. So, it does not seem she did."

"Quite so," said Holmes. "You are, I assume, aware, that the statue has disappeared?"

"Aye, so we have heard. But we have heard neither hide nor hair of where it might have gone. Have you, Mr. Holmes?"

"No. I fear not. But what of the other artifacts you discovered? Anything else of singular value or interest to scholars?"

Again, his question was met by a moment of silence, and the three young fellows glanced at each other. Finally, Cruickshank spoke up.

"You might say, *In mezzo mar siede un paese guasto che s'appella Creta.*"

His colleagues chuckled their approval.

"Perhaps," said Holmes, "instead of showing off your erudition, you might just answer the question."

"Oh, yes, I suppose I could answer in English. As Dante once observed, in the middle of the sea is a wasted island called Crete. That is what we found, Mr. Holmes. You see, the three of us thought the entire expedition was a bust. Arthur Evans and his troop from the Ashmolean had secured the prime location at Knossos and kept pulling up one clay tablet after another. But we were at what must have been a small temple a few miles away. Sure and we found all sorts of shards of pottery and pieces of weapons and the like. The professor kept saying that these were brilliant finds that would unlock volumes of ancient history. But sir, all of us have been studying antiquities for the past six years, and we can tell pretty well if something is a great treasure or a piece of broken trash that had been tossed in the midden. Most of what we found, sir, except for the statue, was not worth a tuppence."

"Oh my," said Holmes. "That must have made the entire time somewhat disappointing."

"Disappointing it was, sir," said Cruickshank. "Bloody frustrating is more like it. You might say we toiled all night and caught nothing."

"I understand," said Holmes, smiling sympathetically. "There have been times when I also worked for weeks on a case and finally had to admit that I had found nothing."

"You don't say, sir," piped up Master Argyle. "In all those stories we have read about you, there wasn't one like that."

"Of course not," said Holmes. "Dr. Watson knows that any account of such a case would disappoint the reader. So those cases are wisely overlooked. Is that not right, Watson?"

I affected a pose of shock and outrage. "Never. I thought all your cases were concluded successfully. As I fully expect this one will be. I am quite sure that one of these fine young chaps has a very good idea of who the culprit was."

"Quite so," agreed Holmes. Then, turning to the three young chaps, he said, "Forgive me if I am being blunt, but I suspect that all of you have thoughts on who may be behind the theft, even if you do not have any idea about the professor's disappearance. Please, speak now."

Again, there was an uncomfortable silence, with none of the fellows willing to speak first. Finally, Cruickshank ventured forth.

"I can say for right sure, Mr. Holmes it was nae one of us."

"I agree. None of you impress me as having the temperament to take such a risk, nor the brains to pull it off without being caught. But you are sufficiently clever to have a reasonably well-founded suspicion."

"If you say so, sir," replied Cruickshank. "Aye, we have a suspicion, sir. For a wee while, not wanting to believe that the professor was dead, we fancied that he might have snuck off the boat and taken Charlotte with him. That was the name he gave to the statue. But that made no sense. We talked it over many times, and now we agree that Lloyd Sunday must have taken the golden cow."

"Thank you, that is helpful. But now you must explain to me why you suspect him."

"Well sir, it was mainly on account of when the baggage was all unloaded off the boat down at the Docklands, there should have been a packing case of the right size to carry the statue of Charlotte, but there was none. The only other place it could have been taken off was when we stopped at Gibraltar. That was where we left Lloyd off as well. So, that's the main reason. And the other part is that we just don't trust him. He was decent to the three of us, but he just seemed to be always hiding something. I cannot say beyond that, Mr. Holmes. It's just that you get a feelin' about some chap and it sticks with you, and all three of us got it."

Holmes continued for some time to cross-question them about Lloyd Sunday, but there was no new data given beyond what I have recorded. Then he changed tack one more time.

"Professor Hume-Craw lived here in St. Andrews, did he not?"

"Aye, he did," they all said and nodded.

"Are his wife and family still living here?"

Cruickshank again took the lead in answering. "That's another hard question to answer. The professor has lived apart from his wife for as long as any of us can remember. She still lives in the town but has a completely different life. His only child that we know of is Miss Gertrude, and she lives in London. Sorry, we canna be of more help to you on that one, sir."

"It is quite all right. You have been very helpful. And I thank you for joining me for the evening."

"Auch, it is us," said young Argyle, "who should be thankin' you, Mr. Holmes. It is a bit rare for us to have a meal like this. So, thank *you*, sir."

The other two added their murmurs of agreement, and they rose and departed into the snowy winter evening.

"Do you believe them?" I asked Holmes after the three fellows were gone and he and I were ensconced in chairs by the fireplace in the parlor.

"Entirely," he replied. "I am quite sure that had I asked them their opinions on Victory at Samothrace, or Venus De Milo, or Myron's Discobolus, or the Rhodian Laocoon, any one of them could have prattled on *ad infinitum ad nauseam*. But otherwise, they are as thick as planks. There is not a shred of evidence of minds clever enough to have undertaken murder and the kidnapping of a priceless artifact."

"The kidnapping?" I queried.

"Oh, Watson. It is elementary. Even a brilliant thief cannot sell a famous work of art or artifact to even a latter-day Jonathan Wild of devious fences. The only way today to profit from such a scheme is to hold the treasured item for ransom. The owner, usually one of our great museums, willingly pays the ransom and sends the bill to Lloyds. Now, my dear doctor, was there anything about those three earnest scholars that would suggest to you that they were capable of undertaking such a scheme?"

I had to admit, that he had adjudicated the fellows' abilities accurately.

"Well then, I said, "it would appear that it was a rather long journey all the way up here for nothing."

"Not at all. Watson. Not at all. Until this evening, they were still on my list of possible suspects. Now they have been eliminated. That is a useful task to have accomplished."

I shrugged and agreed. "Very well, shall we catch the morning train back to Edinburgh?"

"The eleven o'clock train would be better. We have a visit, perhaps two, to make in the morning."

"We do? Where to?"

"Mrs. Hume-Craw, the estranged wife of the recently departed professor, still lives in St. Andrews. I have sent a message to her requesting an interview but have not received a reply as of yet. Professor Hume-Craw had an office at the university, and we shall pay a visit."

"But Holmes, the man is dead. How can you obtain permission to enter his office?"

"If he is dead, Watson. He cannot object."

Chapter Six

The Dead Professor's Office

With the winter solstice just a few weeks past, the daylight hours in St. Andrews are miserably short. When I met Holmes in the breakfast room the following morning, the sun had not yet risen, and a fresh new layer of snow was covering the ground of the first tee of the Old Course. From the inside of the window, it was a lovely site. I was not, however, eager to venture out. Holmes, as I feared was of a different mind.

"Eat up, Watson," he said, smiling. "There is nothing like Scottish oatmeal to prepare you for the day."

To my way of thinking, there was nothing like Scottish oatmeal—a staple on which I had been raised—to make one appreciate Mrs. Hudson all the more.

"What are you going to say," I asked, "if someone stops us and asks why we are breaking into a professor's office?"

"That is highly unlikely, my friend," said Holmes. "Before eight o'clock on a Sunday morning, the only Scots who are awake are dour Presbyterians off to the kirk. The rest will be still recovering from imbibing in too much of their national beverage last evening. Come, fetch your valise and let us be on our way."

Holmes seemed to know his way through the buildings of the old university. This did not come as a surprise. He had a habit of obtaining and memorizing maps of any destination that he might visit, and his memory of every lane and alley in London never ceased to amaze me.

The snow crunched and squeaked beneath our feet as we left our tracks in the virgin blanket of white. There was not a soul in sight, and so, rather than hurrying, I made of point of stopping for just a few seconds and enjoying the emerging faint morning light that was making silhouettes of the ancient buildings.

"This in Hume-Craw's office," said Holmes, after we wandered our way through several corridors and stairwells of one of the academic edifices. He tried the door handle and, to my surprise, it was not locked.

"A trusting lot, these Scotsmen," I whispered.

"Either that," Holmes replied, "or there is nothing in here worth protecting."

Holmes closed the curtains and turned up the lamps. For the next hour, the two of us rifled through the files of the deceased professor. It gave me a queer feeling, something akin to robbing a grave. I voiced my concerns to Holmes who replied as I should have expected.

"I assure you, he is not going to lodge a complaint."

I moved quickly through old lecture notes, and copies of essays and papers submitted by students over the past two decades. I slowed down when I reached the files covering his various summer expeditions to various places in the ancient world.

"Holmes," I said idly as I perused an expense claim file from a past trip to the Greek isles. "What might you expect to pay for a room in a small hotel on the island of Naxos."

"I have not the foggiest notion," he muttered, as he inspected the pages of the files that were in the professor's desk. "Why do you ask?"

"Would you expect the rate to be twenty-two pounds a night?"

He looked up at me. "Good heavens no. I would be surprised if it were more than a pound a night."

"That's what I would have thought. I am no authority on the cost of traveling to the Mediterranean, but it looks to me as if our professor has had a bit of a history of inflating his expenses."

"Are there chits backing up his claims?"

"Yes, mind you, they are all written on the same stock of paper. Not only that, but he seems to have submitted the same claims to two or three different funds, and been paid by all of them."

"How singularly interesting," said Holmes. "You might remove several of the more egregious examples. They could prove useful."

"And what are you finding?" I asked.

"There are several inches of files of correspondence between our man and this Lloyd Sunday fellow. I do not have time to read all of them, but I will take the entire lot with me and look at them on the train."

He returned to his inspection and I to mine.

"Ah, what have we here?" he exclaimed.

"What is it?"

"A thin file of letters—seven of them, the dates are spread over the past fifteen years—all from the office of the Rector of the Ancient University of St. Andrews, in his capacity as the Chairman of the University Court."

"Yes, go on."

He extracted one of them, held it up, and started to read:

"Dear Professor Hume-Craw:
Be assured that the University is most appreciative of your many efforts in securing bequests and other invaluable gifts of ancient artifacts. Kindly take the

following admonishment in light of our gratitude.

We advise that you should not be unmindful of the persistent rumors and two formal complaints made to my office of your ungentlemanly behavior to several of the young women in the stenographic pool.

We trust that you will henceforth govern yourself accordingly.

"There is another letter, some years later, from the office of the Vice-Chancellor that respectfully reminds Professor Hume-Craw that it is not a wise practice to hold meetings with the mothers of students in his office after eight o'clock in the evening."

"I must say," I said, "that our dear departed doctor appears to have been a bit of a cad."

"Indeed, he was."

"But what we have here is a common academic miscreant," I observed. "That is a long stretch short of stealing a priceless gold statue. Do you think he could have had a hand in that before he went for his midnight swim?"

"Anything is possible. It is also possible that whoever else was party to the crime most likely did away with him."

"That tends to point the finger at this fellow Sunday, does it not?"

"Possibly. We must not forget his stocky daughter or even the secretary."

"One of the women?" I asked. "Surely, that is not possible. Even if the secretary were so vile as murder her employer, she could not lift and toss him overboard."

"No, she could not. Not if she were acting alone. Mind you, the daughter could."

We bundled up a selection of the files and departed from the office. At the hotel, a note was waiting at the desk for Holmes. It was a reply from the widow of Professor Hume-Craw. Holmes handed it to me. It ran:

Mr. Sherlock Holmes: I have for reply your note requesting an interview this morning. As I have had nothing whatsoever to do with the affairs of my husband, Professor Edgar Hume-Craw, for the past decade, such a meeting would be a waste of my time and yours.

It was signed 'respectfully' by Mrs. Margaret Hume-Craw.

"As I had expected," said Holmes. "So, come now, Watson. We can begin our reading of files before catching the train."

We took a cab back north to the station in Leuchars and waited inside the station for our train to arrive. Whilst we were waiting, Holmes suddenly stood and looked out the window to the platform. The train from Edinburgh had just pulled in, and the passengers were disembarking.

"Watson, come, please. Do you see that passenger carrying the Gladstone bag?"

I saw to whom he was referring.

"Yes, I do. He is wearing a cassock. Must be a priest. Why?"

"No Watson, *he* is not wearing a cassock. *She* is wearing a dress. Now, does that bring someone to mind?"

I looked again. If it was a woman, then she was far from petite.

"The daughter. Miss Gertrude."

"Precisely. And I suspect that she is on her way to her father's office. Or possibly to visit her lost mother. Perhaps both. It is a good thing that we came and left when we did, else whatever we found might have been long gone."

We both spent the entire journey back to London reading and re-reading the files of the late Professor Hume-Craw. By eleven o'clock in the evening, as we were approaching King's Cross, bleary-eyed, I laid down the last file. Holmes did the same and leaned back and lit a cigarette.

"A penny for your thoughts, Watson," he said.

"Edgar Hume-Craw," I mused, "had an excellent mind, but I had a sense of his playing rather close to the line."

"Ah, how so?"

"He claimed to have made some splendid discoveries throughout the ancient world and published extensively, but on some occasions, the places he claimed to have visited and studied were so remote or in dangerous regions where tribes were battling, that no other scholar has had to opportunity to follow up and continue his work."

"Precisely. And, as a result, no one since has been able to confirm or refute those claims," replied Holmes

"On his Minoan Expedition," I said, "he appears to have finally found the pot of gold at the end of the rainbow. A bit of a shame that he is not alive to enjoy the reward."

"A shame? Yes, I suppose one could say that."

As it was close to midnight when we finally returned to Baker Street, both of us went directly to bed. I fell off to sleep immediately, and I suspect that Holmes did the same.

The next two days passed without incident. On the Tuesday afternoon, I returned to 221B about the same time as did Holmes. Before indulging in something to take away the winter chill, I picked up the small pile of post that had arrived that afternoon.

"Holmes," I said as he poured two snifters of brandy, "You might want to take a look at this one before you attend to our medicinal needs."

I had selected one of the letters. It had the return address of Miss Rowena Ferguson, on Easton Street in Clerkenwell.

"Kindly read it to me whilst I pour," he replied.

I opened the letter and read it aloud.

Dear Mr. Sherlock Holmes.

Words cannot begin to express my gratitude to you, sir. My life has not only been restored to me; it has been blessed beyond all I could ask or imagine. It is all because I followed your advice. In my prayers, I am thanking God every night for a man such as you that Providence led into my life.

After our meeting, I spent an entire night in tears, prayers, anger, and turmoil. The following morning, I rose and realized that my path was set. I would do exactly as you advised. As soon as morning light had come to the streets of London, I went directly to Bernardo's Home and informed the staff that I did not wish my son to be put out for adoption, or shipping off to one of the colonies. I wished to raise him myself, with the help of my family.

I confess that when I made this statement to them, I had not yet secured any response from my family. They knew nothing whatsoever of my fallen condition.

The dear saints at Bernardo's were wonderfully helpful. They not only joyfully returned my son to my care, they gave me an assortment of clothes, blankets and diapers, and even a small basket in which to carry him. I then sent a telegram to my parents telling them that I had earned a bit of a holiday and would be coming to visit. I did not warn them that their grandson would be coming with me.

"Oh my," I interjected, "the Reverend Ferguson is in for a bit of a surprise." I chucked at the prospect and continued to read aloud.

> *It was a long journey, but the other women on the trains were so very helpful, especially after I told them that I was a widow who had lost her husband in the war in the Cape. They offered to look after all my needs, and then some. I told them that I was taking my son for his first visit to his grandparents and that his name was Donald, after his grandfather.*

"A wise young woman," I commented.

"Yes. Very clever. Keep reading," said Holmes.

> *On arriving at the door of my family home in Ayr, I was overcome with fear and was tempted to turn and run away. But I summoned up my courage, said a prayer and waltzed right into my home without even knocking. My mother and father were sitting in their parlor having a cup of tea and in I sauntered. I put the basket with wee Donny in it and cheerfully announced, "Thought you might like to get to know your grandson."*

> *They were speechless, which for a clergyman is a very unusual condition. So, I just told them my story, and when I finished, I waited for their reaction. My mum said nothing, but my father burst into a terrible rage. He stood up, paced the floor, and called me every awful name—all from the Bible—that he could think of. I am sure that some of them would be new even to you, Mr. Holmes.*

My spirit was broken. Yea, crushed. I broke down into tears, and I went to rush out of the room and up to the bedroom that had been mine for my entire life. I did, however, have the presence of mind to lift my son from his basket and, I confess, pretty well throw him into his grandfather's arms. He had no choice but to catch him. I screamed something to the effect of, "Gey weel then, if ye cannae show Christian love tae me, at least ye kinn show it tae the bairnie who bears your name."

Then I ran from the room, up the stairs, slammed closed the door, and flopped on my bed and howled.

I sobbed for at least a half an hour and then there was a knock come to my door. I bade my mother and father enter. My father was still holding his grandson, and wee Donny was fixing his eyes on his grandfather's face, the way infants do. The two of them sat down, and my father quietly said, "It appears that the good Lord in his wisdom has blessed us with a grandson. It has not happened in the manner I might have expected, but it has happened all the same. And sae the Lord be thankit. We shall have to make a few changes but the good Lord gave the Scots the gift of practicality, and so changes we shall make."

I looked at my mother and could see that her heart had turned to mush. My only fear was that my son might have his limbs stretched as the two of them wrestled over who would hold him.

My home became a loving refuge from all the worries of my life in London. Father moved his books and desk out

*of his study and set it up as a nursery. Mother began
straight away to knit and sew clothes for wee Donny.
That Sunday, he preached his homily to the congregation,
and he gave it the title 'Four Hundred and Ninety-One is
an Infinite Number.' That may mean nothing to you, Mr.
Holmes, but it is a reference to the story in the Bible when
Jesus told Peter that he had to keep forgiving his brother.
Without so much as saying it directly, he let the saints in
the pews know that if they did not also forgive me, then
they were transgressing the Word of God. It sufficed.
Mind you, I think it was more as result of their learning
that my fiancée had been a soldier and a fine son of
Scotland, but that mattered not.*

*Then on Sunday afternoon, my father told me that there
was a young man in the congregation, a Mr. Alexander
McTavish, who had asked if he could meet me. He came to
the house later that day and told me his story. His
brother, Robert, had been in the same regiment as my
Archie and had also given his life in the war in the Cape.
Not only that, but he himself was a recent widower. His
wife, Vera, had died giving birth to a baby girl just two
months ago.*

*To my surprise, he looked at me and suggested that the
two of us should consider getting married as it would be
good for his daughter and my son to have both a mother
and a father. I was stunned, but, as my father had said,
the Lord in his wisdom gave we Scots the divine gift of
practicality and so Mr. McTavish, and I had a frank,*

practical discussion and agreed that we should indeed become man and wife.

Andrew is far from the handsome, dashing soldier that Archie was, and I do not have to tell you that I do not feel the rush of passionate love that I had for Archie. But that will come, I hope and pray, in time. Andrew is an accountant and has a solid income and excellent prospects. He already owns a small house in Ayr, and it is no more than twenty minutes away from the home of my family. I am now blessed with a beautiful daughter, and I did not even have to suffer the awful pain of giving birth to her.

So, you see, Mr. Holmes, my life has been completely turned around, and it could not have happened if I had not come to you. If God blesses me in the future with another child and it is a boy, I have determined to name him 'Sherlock.' I hope you will accept my doing so as a small token of my gratitude to you.

"Ah," I sighed. "Can you imagine a happier ending, Holmes?"

"Is that the end?"

"No, there is another paragraph."

"Then keep reading."

I left my son in the care of his grandmother and returned to London yesterday to take care of my affairs here and give fair notice to the Royal Mail of the change in my situation. They have been an honorable employer, and I owe that to them. Before I wrote this letter to you, I wrote out my notice to them, and I wrote one more letter. That was to the vile man who calls himself Charles Augustus Milverton— whoever he may be. I no longer have anything to fear from him. I not only told him in no uncertain words that he could jolly well go to the devil, but that he should find himself a good barrister because I had kept every one of his notes to me and would be taking them straight away to Scotland Yard...

"She *what!!*" shouted Holmes. He jumped out of his chair.

"That naïve young fool," he said. He was pacing the floor, and his eyes were glowing with fear. "She is threatening a murderer."

"How can you say that?" I asked.

"The blackmail scheme at the telegraph office is clearly connected in some way to the disappearance of Professor Hume-Craw. Do not ask me how. I do not yet know. But we are dealing with someone, or some group of people, who were willing to throw a man overboard for the sake of an ancient artifact. They will not think twice of doing harm to Miss Rowena if she has threatened them."

He paced for a few more seconds and then turned to me.

"Her address is on the envelope, is it not?"

"It is. Did you want to ask the police to post a guard?"

"No. There is not time. Grab your coat and your service revolver. We have to get over to her flat at once before they do."

He was already pulling on his winter coat and hat. I ran to my room, grabbed my revolver and a handful of bullets, then my coat, and rushed down the stairs after him.

Chapter Seven
Too Late

Holmes ran into the street and shouted for a cab. He gave the driver the address and added, "And a sovereign if you will gallop all the way."

The driver nodded and laid his whip to the haunches of his horse. He did his best to move as quickly as possible, but it was already dark, and Marylebone and Euston Streets were still busy with pedestrians and carriages. In the recurring light from the street lamps, I caught flashing looks at the face of my friend. He was as distraught as I had ever seen him.

"That innocent naïf," he said, shaking his head. "I warned her not to breathe a word about her blackmailers to anyone, least of all the villain himself. What was she thinking?"

"The pure in heart," I said, "of this world, can be oblivious to the evil in the souls of men that you encounter daily. I am sure she must have thought that since the good Lord brought her such joy with her family in Ayr, He would watch over her in London as well. We shall just have to hope that her faith was well placed."

At the corner of King's Cross, the cab turned right and sped down toward Clerkenwell. After several blocks at full gallop, we took a sharp corner to the left, and then another one. For another few seconds, we raced forward and then came to a full stop.

"Your address," shouted the driver, "is straight ahead. This is as close as I can come."

Holmes leapt out of the cab and tossed a coin up to the driver. I jumped out behind him and then almost ran into his body. He had stopped and was standing still, looking ahead. Two police carriages blocked the street in front of the house where Miss Rowena Ferguson lived.

"Dear God, no," muttered Holmes. Then he began to walk toward the front door. Two constables were standing on the small porch, and one of them nodded and greeted Holmes by name. In the entryway, a smaller man turned to us as we entered.

"Hello Holmes," said Inspector Lestrade. "I just sent a man to fetch you. Not surprised to see you here, though. Come in. Was she a client of yours?"

I could feel my heart sink as we entered a tiny flat on the far side of the ground floor. Once inside, my worst fears were realized. In the bedroom, in a chair in front of a small dressing table and mirror, was the lifeless body of a young woman. She was clad in only her undergarments with her head drooping down on her chest. Her corset and the floor beneath her was covered in dark blood that had gushed from her throat. I knew immediately that a few hours earlier, someone had cut the throat of Miss Rowena Ferguson.

I felt Holmes's hand on my forearm. For several seconds he gripped me like an iron vice. I brought my other hand across my body and placed it on top of his. Slowly the grip relaxed, and he let go.

"Inspector," he said, "could you please impart to me such information as you have so far?"

"Right. On her table, you can see a packet of postage stamps. Beside it was a note bearing the name and address of Mr. Sherlock Holmes. Other than that, nothing else has been disturbed. The poor lass is in exactly the position she was when she was found. Her landlady knocked on her door an hour or so ago. Seems the young lady had invited her out for dinner as some sort of celebration. When Miss Ferguson, who she said was always as punctual as Big Ben, did not come by her door after a half hour had past the agreed time, she came and knocked. The door was open, and she came in and found her here just as she is. She ran out and called for the police. First, the local constable came in and then he sent for me. I arrived some twenty minutes back. Soon as I saw your name, I sent for you.

"As far as we can tell," continued Lestrade, "some villain must have gained entry through the kitchen window. It was sitting open and still is. And he must had snuck up behind her and killed her and then ran out the door, leaving it open. That's all we can put together so far."

"That appears to be reasonable," said Holmes. His voice was quiet, and his face was pale. "Might I, with your permission Inspector, examine the rooms?"

"Please do, Holmes. And then let us know your thoughts. We know that you sometimes have insights that we might not, so, do proceed."

For the next half hour, Holmes inspected the small flat that Miss Rowena Ferguson had called her home for the past two years. He slowly looked through her closets and wardrobes, her small kitchen, the cluster of bottles on her dressing table, the hairbrush on the coffee table, her wooden case of writing paper, pens and inks, and her single shelf of books. In so many previous instances when Holmes conducted his close examination of the site of a murder, he moved with energy and determination. On that day, he was listless, moving slowly as if in pain. His heart was not in it.

"I agree with your analysis, Inspector," he said after completing the task. "Your conclusion, for quite obvious reasons, that her killer most likely entered through the window and approached unseen from behind her has some merit. My suggestion is that you immediately send a notice to all available inspectors and constables to look for a man by the name of Lloyd Sunday. On Friday evening, he resided at the Alpha Inn in Bloomsbury. It had been my intention to accost him there on Saturday morning. However, I changed my plans, most unfortunately it now appears. I am certain that your men can track him down from there."

"You believe," asked Lestrade, "that he is the killer?"

"Of that, I am not yet certain. I do have reason to believe that he is connected in some way both to this dreadful crime and to the disappearance of Professor Hume-Craw."

"Very well, Holmes. I will put out the notice straight away, but you best sit down and explain to me what this is all about."

The three of us found a small pub back out on Farringdon Road and Holmes methodically expounded to Inspector Lestrade the elements of the case to date and whatever evidence he had already discovered and deduced.

"Right, so you are telling me, Holmes, that there has been an organized cabal of spies inside the Royal Mail telegraph center, that whoever is behind that ring discovered that there is some priceless gold statue found in Crete, that the statue was stolen and could perhaps be somewhere between London and Gibraltar, and that people are being murdered because of it, and that some chap named Sunday is our best lead. Is that correct, Holmes?"

"That is a reasonable summary," said Holmes.

"Right, so who are these spies reporting to?" asked Lestrade. "You and I both know that when a gang of small fry are working together, there is always a puppet master somewhere in the wings."

Holmes was silent for a moment before answering. "It is highly likely, Inspector, that you are correct. However, at present, I do not know. An answer will have to wait for the morrow when far more data has been acquired. The Good Lord Himself admonished us that sufficient unto the day is the evil thereof."

We hailed a cab and began the journey back to Baker Street. The look I had observed so many times in the past, the keenness of Holmes's eyes, and the determined set of his jaw, were nowhere to be seen. On three occasions he dropped his face into his hands and slowly shook his head. Twice, I heard the barely audible words, "I should have known."

Holmes said nothing to me after we returned to 221B. He poured himself a snifter of brandy and went straight into his room. For the next two nights, he was gone. I could tell that he had been back to our rooms when I returned from my medical practice, but there was no note and no explanation. Mrs. Hudson reported that she had heard him arrive and then leave again a half hour later.

It was not until the evening of the following day that I returned to Baker Street and found Holmes sitting by the fire in his dressing gown and puffing on his beloved pipe. Without speaking, he gestured first to the decanter of brandy on the mantle, and then to my familiar chair across from him. I poured myself a glass and sat down.

He took several more languorous drafts on his pipe before saying anything.

"The past few days," he said, "have been a bit of a tough go on my spirits."

"I can see that, my friend. However, your excellent mind cannot possibly predict the unforeseeable."

"You are quite right, my friend. And I am sure that there have been days in your medical career that one of your patients died who could, in hindsight, have been saved had you acted differently."

I sighed. "Yes. There have been several. It is part of the life of every doctor. We do the best we can with the knowledge we have at the time. I fear it has been the same for you."

He took another slow draft. "I fear it has."

This comment was followed by yet several more puffs. I had seldom before Holmes before in such a melancholy mood, and I merely sat and attentively waited for his next words.

"On those sad days, my friend," he asked, "do you unburden yourself to your dear wife as soon as you return home?"

"Of course. I cannot imagine how I could survive otherwise. Her loving attentiveness and embrace revive my soul and spirit and make it so much easier to carry on."

"Quite so. I have perceived that you, like the poet, after becoming married were surprised by joy."

"Indeed, I was."

"However, you would not call me a marrying man, Watson?"

"No, indeed."

"You will be interested to know that I am contemplating it."

For a moment, I was speechless, and then I became fearful.

"Holmes," I asked, "are you contemplating marriage with the person I think you are?"

"If you are referring to Miss Lightowlers, then yes."

I could not restrain myself. "Holmes," I gasped, "I can see that you are distraught, but have you also taken complete leave of your senses?"

"Not at all, my friend. Over the past few days, you know how deeply my spirit has been vexed. After a full day of fruitless investigating, attempting in vain to atone for my dreadful mistake that allowed the death of that poor young woman, I have enjoyed the revival of my life force that spending time in the company of a highly intelligent, informed, and caring woman brings."

"And beautiful."

"Of course. You yourself could not help but notice how just gazing at her brings a certain pleasure to the soul."

"I am well acquainted with the malady, Holmes. I have had it recounted to me more times than I can remember from starry-eyed men sitting in my office. There is no known cure, but fortunately, the fever does not last long. I expect that yours will break soon and a full recovery will be had."

"Do you truly believe that, my dear doctor," asked Holmes.

"Indeed, I do," I said, with feigned confidence.

Chapter Eight
Un Excellent Déjeuner
Français

I slept little that night. As I tossed and turned and mentally wrestled with what Holmes had said, a growing conviction slowly came over me. Holmes needed my care. I was his personal physician, and he needed my protection. I had no choice but to take action and first thing in the morning, I entered the fray.

Before Holmes had arisen, I had penned a note, descended to Baker Street, and summoned one of the Irregulars. A sleepy-eyed lad appeared in response to my whistle, and I gave him a letter addressed to Miss Ruth Lightowlers. I insisted on meeting her for lunch and informed her that I would be waiting for her at noon at a small café near the delta of Islington Green and Upper Street. I was quite determined to give the young woman a piece of my mind, and, for her own good, make it abundantly clear that marrying Sherlock Holmes was not at all in her best interests. Furthermore, it would be a great loss to the safety of the citizens of London if his extraordinary talents were to be diverted away from the singular attention to the pursuit of justice.

I had chosen a select restaurant that had a reputation for being discriminating in its clientele and offering an excellent if pompously expensive menu. I admit that I hoped my guest would find it somewhat intimidating. At eleven o'clock, I postponed all my appointments until later in the afternoon and took a cab to Islington. By twenty minutes to noon, I was seated at a table. My stomach was in knots as I rehearsed the remarks I was about to deliver, and as I attempted to predict every possible reply that Miss Lightowlers might make and my response in turn.

One of the advantages that years of medical practice bestows upon a man, unwelcomed though it may be, is the immunity to the bewitching effect that a woman's physical beauty has on the rest of the male half of the human race. A female body may be as perfect as Aphrodite's but when it's various leaky orifices are routinely poked and prodded, it loses it magical charms. Listening to a recitation of the problems of bowel movements is not known to lead to a pleasant hormonal response from the attendant male. And there is absolutely nothing on earth so *un*likely to move a man to swoon at a woman's beauty than delivering a baby from her womb. I was, therefore, not worried in the least of being charmed into irrationality by the lovely Miss Lightowlers.

At precisely twelve noon, I saw her come through the door. Were I not a medical man, I might have responded in the same way the maitre d' and the waiters did as this remarkably beautiful woman walked toward my table, smiling at every man she passed and, no doubt, turning their knees to putty.

"Why Dr. Watson," she said, as she approached my table and confidently held out her hand to me, "this is such a splendid surprise. Did Mr. Holmes suggest this lovely restaurant? It is my favorite in all of north London. Why he and I had a splendid dinner together here just two nights ago. And now a delightful lunch with another famous and accomplished man. I am honored and thrilled beyond words, sir."

A part of my plan had immediately vanished, but I smiled, lifted her hand a modest direction toward me, and bade her be seated.

From her handbag, she immediately withdrew a copy of my most recently published book, a collection of the adventures of Sherlock Holmes that had appeared in the Strand over the past year.

"Oh, Dr. Watson, you must think me just a foolish girl, but I could not resist the opportunity. I have read all of your stories over and over again, and I beg you, sir, do me the honor of signing my copy of this book."

I fumbled to retrieve my pen and asked one of the waiters to bring over a bottle of ink. He did so, arriving with a choice bottle of claret in his hand. He made a shallow bow toward my guest.

"May I presume that the lady would enjoy a glass of her favorite?"

"Oh, Sebastian," she replied, beaming at him, "you do such a brilliant job of looking after me. I do not know how I would get through a meal without you."

Before I could introduce any topic for conversation, she, with a coy smile, began a series of highly informed questions about the books and stories I had published. Although whatever reputation I had acquired was entirely the result of my accounts of the adventures of Sherlock Holmes, I had also published several other stories and books, none of which had sold many copies. Miss Lightowlers, however, had read them all. Not only so, but her knowledge seemed remarkably thorough and her questions quite brilliantly insightful. When the maitre d' approached the table she immediately made sure he knew who I was.

"My dear Jean-Paul," she said, "did you know that the most successful writer in all of London is here today? This is the famous Dr. John Watson. His books have sold literally thousands of copies all over the Empire, and even in America."

She went on with such fulsome praise that I felt a blush coming to my face.

Effortlessly, she took control of the conversation, and ever so subtly making certain that I felt very good about myself in her company. I was beginning to see how even Sherlock Holmes might have fallen for her charms.

Finally, after the excellent main course had been cleared away, I took advantage of her pausing to take a swallow of claret, and turned the conversation to my reason for meeting with her. Patiently, but forcefully I expressed to her my concerns over the obvious infatuation that my friend, Sherlock Holmes had developed for her. When I paused, hoping that a moment of silence would enhance the serious tenor of my remarks, she smiled at me in a most loving howbeit condescending manner.

"Oh, my dear doctor. You are so very kind and thoughtful to take time away from all the important things you are doing to think of my best interests, and those of your dear, dear friend. But I assure you that I am completely certain that whatever interest Mr. Sherlock Holmes has in me is no more than as a plaything for his amusement. I enjoy his attention and am in awe of his brilliant mind, but I expect that he will soon tire of me and move on. I am sure you have seen this all before with any number of eligible unmarried women."

"No, Miss, I have not. Sherlock Holmes has, for the more than twenty years I have known him, shown no interest whatsoever in any romantic attraction to any woman. You are most assuredly the first."

I went on at some length to repeat the point I had just made, and even went so far as to list off, without giving full names, several of the exceptional women whom Holmes had encountered over the years. Not one of them, I pronounced, had had any effect on him at all. Then I dropped the cannonball onto the table.

"He has confided in me that he is planning on asking you to marry him."

My statement had its desired effect. Her eyes went wide and her mouth opened in shock. An involuntary blush appeared in her uniquely beautiful face.

I then carried on with the remainder of my prepared speech, carefully and sensitively listing off all the irrefutable reasons why such a course of action would be disastrous both for her and for Holmes. When I came to the end of my discourse, it occurred to me that for the past few minutes she had not been listening to me at all. Her gaze had gone to some indeterminate spot partway between my left ear and the ceiling. Her entire countenance looked unmistakably rapturous.

"Sherlock Holmes wants to marry me?" she said, in dreamlike tones.

"Yes, Miss Lightowlers, that is what I said." I was about to repeat my most salient point when she merely repeated.

"Sherlock Holmes ... wants to marry ... me?"

She brought her gaze back down out of the clouds.

"Forgive me, Dr. Watson. It is just that I find that difficult to comprehend."

I bit my tongue to avoid blurting out something to the effect of *well you bloody well should. It is utter madness.*

Instead, I tactfully replied, "I find it that way myself, Miss. However, I assure you … I would swear an oath in court were we in one … that what I have told you is God's truth."

She dropped her gaze down to her left hand and opened up the fingers and smiled. In not much above a whisper, she muttered. "Mrs. Sherlock Holmes." Then a slow smile began to creep across her face. There was a fleeting second when I thought it was developing into a wicked grin, but then her lovely face took on a glowing radiance.

"My dear, dear Dr. Watson. How can I ever thank you? Had you come to warn me that Sherlock Holmes was doing no more than teasing me with his attention, and warned me against believing his protestations, I would not have been surprised, and I would have shared a pleasant laugh with you over the absurdity of the entire episode. But you are telling me, and I can see that you are doing so in utmost sincerity, that this most incredible of men deems me worthy to fall in love with and wishes to marry. What can I say, doctor? I am left speechless."

Now I was speechless. This was not the reaction I had hoped and carefully planned to engender. Before I could recover my wits the stunningly beautiful young woman rose, came over to where I was sitting, leaned down and planted a light kiss on my cheek. She thanked me yet again and floated out of the restaurant. She smiled at the men and thanked the maitre d' on the way.

"You are always welcome, Mademoiselle B," he said in reply.

For several seconds, I sat in dumb amazement. Then, rather suddenly, something hit me like a jolt of lightning.

What did he just call her? Mademoiselle B?

I quickly paid the outrageous bill and sauntered, as nonchalantly as I could, up to the maitre d'.

"Quite the lovely woman, is she not?" I said.

"Mais oui, monsieur. She is très *gor-guuuzzz*."

"Does Mademoiselle B come here often?" I asked casually.

I saw a quick flicker in his eyes, and he turned to me and offered a Gallic shrug.

"Qui, monsieur? Ah, you mean Mademoiselle Ruth. Oui, de temps en temps. But always it is a pleasure to have her grace our table. But of course, it is also a grand honneur to have with us the famous writer, Dr. Watson. You must come again, monsieur."

I assured him I would though I considered it highly unlikely. A spark had been lit in my brain by his careless parting remark to my guest. Something that had made me uneasy from the very moment she waltzed into 221B Baker Street was now crystallizing. This woman who had so bewitched even Sherlock Holmes could not fool me. No. She was an imposter, and if even Holmes could not see through her, I was determined to unmask her, expose her trickery, and bring my friend back to his senses.

But how?

I began to walk south on Upper Street, pondering my next course of action. Then suddenly, the solution presented itself to me. I hailed a cab.

"Harley Street," I shouted to the driver. "Corner of New Cavendish."

Chapter Nine
Dead Men Tell No Tales

Amongst the gentlemen of the medical profession, it is an inviolable rule that confidences entrusted to us by our patients must never be discussed outside of the walls of the our offices and hospitals. I had never, in over two decades of being a close friend of Sherlock Holmes, disclosed to him any information about one of my patients, not even in those rare situations when doing so might have been useful to him in the solving of a case. I was highly circumspect even in my conversations with my dear wife. I might talk about some unusual or amusing exchange I had had during the day, but I had never disclosed the name of the person whose health and well-being had been confidentially entrusted to me.

However, when medical men came together, knowing that the outside world had been excluded, we were as chatty as a parish sewing circle. Complaints were shared. Tales of woe were commiserated over. Outrageously funny events were recounted and greeted with guffaws and tears of laughter. Knowing this, I proceeded directly to the office of Dr. Lomaga, the highly respected expert in the care of the skin. Miss Ruth, or whatever her name was, had disclosed that she had been to see him. I was reasonably sure that he would know far more about her than had been disclosed to me or to Sherlock Holmes.

The highly-regarded doctor had built up a prosperous practice amongst the upper classes of London who could pay to have the onset of wrinkles and sagging epidermis postponed. His waiting room was full of women of a certain age, all finely dressed and several accompanied by animals that were about the size of sewer rats but were classed as lap dogs. I gave a note to his nurse and waited for him to dispose of his current patient before being ushered into his office.

"John Watson!" he exclaimed. "What a treat. Welcome, my dear chap. To what do I owe this honor?"

He shook my hand vigorously and bade me be seated.

"I am in need of your help, doctor," I said. "However, I fear I cannot completely disclose the reasons."

I knew that would grab his attention.

"A case for Sherlock Holmes?" he asked, eagerly.

"Quite so."

I confess that I had become something of an object of envy amongst the doctors of London. Whilst they toiled endlessly in their surgeries and hospital visits, I had the splendid opportunity from time to time to race all over creation with Sherlock Holmes as we pursued and apprehended one dangerous criminal after another. I dare say that some of my medical brethren engaged in vicarious adventures through me. Without fail, whenever I suggested to any one of them that he might assist in some small way, they were eager to help. I could be counted on to include their names in my acknowledgments, which ensured that they bought multiple copies of the story for distribution to their family and friends and for the reading tables in their waiting rooms.

"I am in need," I said, with a sincere, imploring look on my face, "of some information about one of your recent patients."

"By all means. Which one?"

"I am not entirely sure of her name. She has been using the name of Ruth Lightowlers of late, but I suspect that it is to hide her true identity."

"No one by that name has come by recently. Searching my memory, I cannot recall a patient by that name ever coming to see me. Can you describe her?"

"She would have been here in the past two to three weeks and possibly presented as a case of eczema on the back and sides of her neck."

"There have been three such cases come through here recently. Pray, describe her appearance. Young, old? Slender, well-fed?" What did she look like?"

"Red hair. Irish complexion. Stunningly beautiful."

"Ha. That would be Miss Bernadette O'Donohue," he said. "Yes, quite the beauty, isn't she? But it was not eczema. She had a common sunburn. I am always telling those with red hair and pale skin that they must keep the sun off of their skin. They are terribly susceptible to the ultra-violet rays. Yes, that young woman had a bit of a problem, but I gave her some aloe, and it appears to have cleared things up. No lasting damage to such a lovely neck."

"A sunburn? How in heaven's name did she acquire a sunburn in England in winter time?"

"Oh, she was not in England. She had been working out of doors somewhere in the Mediterranean. Some manner of archeological expedition, she said. Quite the adventurous type, she is."

It would have been very rude for me to leap to my feet and rush out of his office and hail the nearest cab. So, I chatted on for a few more minutes and then, apologizing for taking his valuable time away from his patients, I took my leave.

"Anytime, Watson, old chap," he said. "Made my day to think I might help Sherlock Holmes. Anytime."

Having departed his office, I then ran to the nearest cab and barked an order to get me over to Baker Street on the double.

On arriving, I leapt from the cab, bounded across the pavement, and then in seven vigorous steps ascended our stairs. I threw open the door to our rooms and beheld Holmes sitting by the fire in his dressing gown, puffing absently on his pipe.

"Holmes!" I shouted. "You have been played the fool."

He looked at me without any evidence of alarm at what I had just said.

"Ah, my dear Watson. Do take your coat off and sit down. And pray tell me, how was your luncheon at *Chez Henri*. Did you have the house specialty, the *canard a l'orange*? Ah, perhaps that is a bit heavy for a noon meal. The *sole meuniere* perhaps? And I do hope you had a pleasant conversation with the lovely young lady. You will have to become used to seeing her around quite often in the near future as I expect that after the wedding she will be moving in here with me. I had thought of looking for another flat that was in a more desirable neighborhood, but I fear I am just too set in my ways to vacate Baker Street."

"How in heaven's name could you possibly have known where I was?" I demanded.

"My dear friend, if you are going to leave your Kelly's Directory of London open on the side table with a note of the address of a restaurant on top of the page, then knowing such a fact is not particularly difficult. And as it is a favorite of Miss Lightowlers, I assumed that you had enjoyed her company whilst there."

"Very well, then, Holmes. But that woman, Miss Lightowlers, is an imposter."

He smiled and took another puff on his pipe.

"I presume you are referring to Miss Bernadette O'Donohue of the O'Donohues of Donnybrook in Dublin. The one who was the personal secretary to our dear departed professor on the expedition to Crete?"

I was stunned. "You *know* that about her? How could you *possibly* have known that?"

"My dear doctor, what do you think a detective does when in a lady's private flat and she excuses herself to use the lavatory. You very quickly rifle through every possible drawer, file, cupboard, ashtray, and wardrobe available and learn as much as you can as quickly as possible. Please, Watson, it is quite elementary."

"Does she know that you know?"

"Of course not. The young woman is living in fear. Two people who had some connection to the Minoan Expedition are already dead. She is obviously seeking the type of protection that she believes I can afford her, and I am, I confess, quite honored and pleased to provide it for her."

"Holmes, quite frankly, that is madness. If she is in danger, she will remain so even if you marry her."

"Oh no, I think not. I am looking into a property in Sussex to which I might retire. Perhaps I could become a country gentleman and keep bees. The two of us could live together in a bee-loud glade. Does that not strike you as a consummation devoutly to be wished?"

I starred at Holmes for several more seconds, shook my head, turned and descended the stairs. I would spend the remainder of the day attending to my patients and not wasting any more time.

When I returned to 221B in time for dinner, Holmes was not present. I poured myself a small glass of sherry and sat and waited for him. Some fifteen minutes later I heard the door and his familiar steps on the stairs. He entered and slowly removed his winter coat and sat down. He looked thoroughly weary and such a far cry from what I had seen earlier in the day. I rose and poured out another glass of sherry and handed it to him.

"Ah, thank you, my friend'" he said. "Your thoughtfulness and the prospect of an enjoyable dinner help to revive the spirit."

"Care to tell me what you have doing that has left you looking so bone-weary?"

"I have spent the entire afternoon dogging the footsteps of Mr. Lloyd Sunday. It has all been in vain."

"Did you find his lodgings?"

"Yes, he stayed two nights ago in Halliday's Private Hotel in Euston. A few of his belongings are still there, but the desk assured me that he did not sleep in his room last night and has not been seen all day. He has vanished once more."

"And have you concluded," I asked, "that he is the key to unraveling this mystery?"

"Of his exact actions with respect to the deaths of the professor and poor Miss Rowena, I am not entirely clear, but I am certain that he is involved. He also presents a significant danger to Miss Lightowlers, or Miss O'Donohue as we now know her to be."

"Is Lestrade looking for him as well?"

"He has assigned several men to the task."

"Very well then, Holmes, you may as well let them prowl the streets of London whilst you enjoy your dinner."

Holmes did not enjoy his dinner. Mrs. Hudson served up a fine supper of lamb chops, but Holmes picked away at them in a desultory manner. His mind was elsewhere.

Mrs. Hudson had no sooner cleared away the table when a knock came to the door. Then the door opened without anyone going to see who had arrived, and we heard a set of footsteps ascending the stairs.

"Hmm," muttered Holmes. "Inspector Lestrade. I wonder what news he brings."

Lestrade was by now very familiar with the rooms at 221B Baker Street, and he took off his winter coat and walked directly to his usual place on the sofa.

"I heard that Sherlock Holmes was all over London looking for Mr. Lloyd Sunday," said Lestrade.

"Indeed, I was," replied Holmes. "My path crossed more than once with your men."

"Well, you will be pleased to know that we found him. Might you be interested in coming to meet him?"

"Indeed, I would," said Holmes. "Are you holding him at a station or at the offices of the Yard?"

"Neither. We're holding him at the Tower Bridge. In Dead Man's hole."

"The morgue?"

"That is the customary place for holding bodies we fish out of the river, is it not?"

"Indeed, it is," said Holmes.

"Well then, come along. Don't expect to learn much. As they say, dead men tell no tales. And Dr. Watson, please join us. Your medical expertise would be helpful."

Chapter Ten
The Bird Has Flown

Themagnificent Tower Bridge, spanning the Thames from the Tower of London across to Potters Fields opened about ten years ago. For reasons known only to those responsible for its design and construction, a mortuary was built into the north tower and was quickly given the name of Dead Man's Hole. On average, two or three bodies a week would be fished out of the water and brought to this dungeon-like setting and dried out. They would be left there until identified and delivered to the next-of-kin or, if unclaimed, buried in a pauper's grave.

The three of us rode in Lestrade's police carriage all the way across London from Marylebone, through the City, and over to the Tower. In the early winter evening, there was little light from the streetlights as we hurried through the streets.

"He arrived here yesterday," said Lestrade as we descended from the roadway to the mortuary. "One of my lads thought to come and look for him here and found his name stitched into his suit jacket. The morticians said that he was in the water less than an hour. Some fishermen heard a shot near the Bar of Gold and found him. Still bleeding but quite dead."

The rooms of the Hole were adequately lit but poorly ventilated, and the place stank with a mixture of death and preservative chemicals. The officials assigned to this dismal location peeled back the sheet from a body that was lying on one of the several tables. On it was a man of about forty years of age. He was well-dressed and appeared fit and healthy. Lestrade pulled back the heavy overcoat and his suit jacket, exposing his white shirt underneath. There was a pinkish blotch that extended from his sternum to his navel. The blood had been washed away in part by the water of the Thames, but there was no mistaking the fact that he had either been shot or stabbed in the heart.

"Take a look, gentlemen," said Lestrade. "And then give me your thoughts."

Holmes extracted his glass and began a slow, methodical examination of the body, beginning with his shoes and working his way up. I opened the shirt and looked immediately at the mortal wound.

When Holmes had completed his examination, he turned to me.

"Yes, doctor, what are your conclusions?"

"A revolver shot directly to the heart," I said. "Without extracting the bullet, I could not say precisely what caliber of gun was used, but just by the size of the hole, it was in the range used by the army. My guess would be a Webley Bulldog. There are many of them all over London, as they were issued to the fellows fighting in the Cape. One shot was all it took since it plugged him right in the heart. He would have died within a minute. The killer was a crack shot. Either that or only a few inches away."

"The latter," said Holmes. "To be more precise, the gun was held directly against his chest before being fired. You can tell by the residue of the gunpowder. Even though much of it was washed away, enough remains to indicate a point-blank distance. The powder had not spread more than a quarter of an inch from the center of the hole in his shirt."

"Right," said Lestrade. "So, it looks to me as if some bloke surprised him, held a revolver up to his chest, backed him up to the edge of the quay, and let him have it."

"Perhaps," said Holmes. "There is some reddening on his cheek that does not look faded. What of that?"

"Right. The killer gave him a left hook to the face and then stuck the gun in his chest."

"Ah, yes. Of course," said Holmes. "No doubt, that is what must have happened."

"Good. Now that we have found your number one suspect, Holmes, where do you go from here?" demanded Lestrade.

"With your permission," said Holmes. "I will search his pockets and then the last hotel room he was known to have rented and see if, perchance, he left any clues behind. Would that be acceptable to you, Inspector?"

"Right. Go ahead. But let me know if you find anything that indicates anything."

"Of course, Inspector."

I had not been inside Halliday's Private Hotel for many years. Oddly enough, it was also the final hotel used by Joseph Stangerson some two decades ago in the very first story I recorded of the adventures of Sherlock Holmes. Back then the Boots had nearly fainted at the sight of a stream of blood seeping out from under the door. On this occasion, however, there was no blood and no body to be found inside the room. There were two steamer trunks and a closet full of men's clothes. Holmes and I carefully went through every drawer, pocket, envelope, cigarette case, and pair of shoes in search of anything that would help us to identify not only the killer but also his motive. Nothing struck me as of particular interest, but in a plain brass cigarette case, somewhat crushing a cluster of Taddy's Navy Cut, Holmes found a small key.

"Ha," he said. "What have we here? A key to a luggage locker, with the number stamped on it. How very useful, would you not agree, Watson?"

"Useful," I said, "if we knew in which of several score of train and Underground stations the locker was in."

"I will think that one over," said Holmes. "But now, we may as well return to Baker Street and importune Mrs. Hudson for a late dessert which can be augmented by glass or two of claret."

The following morning, I emerged from my room to find Holmes already seated at the table and enjoying his morning cup of tea.

"Good morning, Watson," he said. "I trust you slept well. We have a short journey ahead of us immediately you have finished your breakfast."

"Where to?"

"London Cannon Street."

"You have concluded that the locker for which we have the key is there?"

"I have indeed. It is the closest train station to the spot along the Thames where poor Mr. Sunday met his watery demise. It is also where one boards the boat trains over to Europe. Anyone who disembarked a boat from Crete in Marseilles would have arrived in England at that station. I cannot say with a certainty until we go and visit, but at the moment it appears to be the most likely."

I had no reason to question Holmes's reasoning and, as soon as I had finished my breakfast, we set out across town one more time. The newsboys were already on the streets and shouting about the murder of Mr. Lloyd Sunday and, in colorful language, describing his death from a sharpshooter who had popped one right into his heart.

Cannon Street is not as large as Waterloo or Victoria, but it is a busy little place all the same. Railway cars are shunted from land onto a set of rails inside the ferry and, several hours later, are pushed off and onto a set of rails that run to the docks in Calais. With hundreds of passengers coming and going from the Continent, it was to be expected that there would be an ample supply of luggage lockers. Indeed, there were several hundred.

All we had to do was find the one whose number corresponded to the key we had found in Lloyd Sunday's room and see if it opened. We found the locker within five minutes. It was one of the largest available to travelers, but there was no need to bother inserting the key.

The door of the locker was already open. I could see immediately that it had been pried with a jimmy and forced.

"I fear we are too late," I said, stating the obvious.

Holmes immediately bent down and peered inside the locker.

"It is still full of cases and a valise. Here, kindly take these as I pull them out and lay them on the floor."

He first pulled out a wooden packing case, followed by a small truck, and finally a valise. All had a baggage tag affixed to them, and they all had the name of Lloyd Sunday inscribed. I set them on the floor beside the bank of lockers and, as they were not locked, opened them.

"Are we looking for a priceless Charlotte?" I asked.

Holmes mumbled something and began to inspect what had been retrieved from the locker. Piece by piece he extracted cameras, tripods, photographic plates, rolls of artists' canvas and craft paper, tubes of paint, colored chalks, and the like.

"As I feared," he said. "Everything here is related to Mr. Sunday's job on the expedition. I will have it all sent over to Scotland Yard for inspection and the developing of any plates that were used on the project. But I suspect that there is nothing here of significant value. There was enough room in the locker for another case containing a small statue. Our Charlotte appears to have trotted off to greener pastures."

We returned to Baker Street in time for a pleasant lunch, again provided by the indomitable Mrs. Hudson. We were just finishing our tea when the afternoon post arrived. I sorted through it and selected one letter that was of obvious interest.

"A personal letter for you, Holmes," I said. "Going by the return address, it might even be a love letter."

The address was written in a feminine hand, and the fine ivory-colored paper had a distinct perfumed scent to it. The return address in the corner indicated that the letter was from Miss Ruth Lightowlers, with a postal box number in the E.C. I announced the sender and handed it over to Holmes, who was trying to appear quite nonchalant about it.

"Another one? Very well, do hand it over. The dear young lady is quite the correspondent, I must say."

He stretched out his long arm and took the letter. In a desultory manner, he slowly opened and read it. As he did so, I observed the smile vanishing from his face and a deep scowl appearing. When he had finished, he threw the letter onto the side table, and I could swear that I hear the words, "damn and blast" escape his lips. For the next few minutes, he said nothing and sat with his hands together below his chin, fingertips touching.

Slowly a smile returned to his face, and he turned to me.

"Watson did not the Bard remind us that 'Frailty, thy name is woman?'"

"He did." I was tempted to remind him that Hamlet said it of his mother and that it might not be applicable to Miss Lightowlers/O'Donohue.

"It appears that the lovely young woman who has captured my heart is subject to the timorous and illogical reactions that are so characteristic of her sex. Here, kindly read this and give me your insights."

He handed the note over to me. It was written in a polished hand, and it ran:

My dearest Sherlock:

It is with the greatest force of my will that I bid my heart be still whilst I write this letter to you. Words cannot express my profound gratitude for the interest and affection you have shown me. Your dear friend, Dr. Watson, has convinced me that your feelings toward me are sincere and unfeigned and I am beyond ecstasy in knowing that I have become the object of your love.

However, a great misfortune has befallen me. I have, just yesterday, read in the newspaper of the terrible murder of the man who once had promised me his undying love and who breached his promise. My soul has been wracked with fear for my own life. Whoever killed him might also wish to kill me. I have no choice but to go into hiding until the murderer is apprehended.

While I am comforted by your profession of affection and the offer of your protection, nevertheless—and please forgive my doubting nature—I am tormented by nagging doubts of your intentions. You have yet to bring up the possibility of marriage in our delightful conversations, and I cannot help but wonder if your desire for my companionship is a fleeting amusement.

Therefore, I must take steps for my own well-being and remove myself from the public eye for the foreseeable future. You may, if you should so wish, contact me by way of the mail forwarding service I am using. I will have no fixed address for the time being and will, of necessity, make my whereabouts unknown and unknowable. I do trust that you will understand and forgive my fearful spirit.

Be assured that I will once again reach out to you as soon as my safety has been secured.

Yours very truly,

"Well, Holmes," I said. "Your pretty bird appears to have flown the coup."

He did not reply. He was pacing the floor back and forth, obviously agitated. For a minute he stopped and stared out the bay window and slowly and purposefully took out a cigarette and inhaled. As he did so, his body appeared to relax, and the scowl on his face was replaced once again by a serene smile. He turned, came back to where I was sitting and sat down facing me.

"My dear friend," he said. "For twenty years or more you have been my faithful Boswell. Now I am in need of you to play another role."

"Yes?"

"I need you, my friend, to be my Cyrano?"

"Your what?"

"Not my *what*, Watson, my *who*."

"Very well, then ... who?"

"My Cyrano. Surely you recall the story of Cyrano de Bergerac. He was wonderfully gifted with a pen and with his tongue, and he gave to Christian the words needed to woo the beautiful Roxanne."

"Yes, yes. I know the story, Holmes. But what in heaven's name has it to do with me?"

"My dear Watson. I acknowledge that I have many unique talents, but the ability to speak or write words of love to a fair maiden is quite beyond me. I need you to compose a letter to Miss Lightowlers ..."

"You mean Miss O'Donohue."

"If you insist, yes. But as she is not yet aware that both of us have unmasked her hidden identity, we must continue to use her pseudonym. What I am in desperate need of is for you to write her a letter not only affirming my love for her but convincing her that I wish to be married to her at the earliest possible date; before the end of the week. I have decided that I cannot possibly live without her. Will you do that for me? I am beseeching you on the basis of our friendship for so many years. I am in need of your help, Watson. Can I count on you?"

Merciful heavens, I thought to myself. In years gone by, Sherlock Holmes had asked me to help him by engaging in actions that were on the wrong side of the law, to help apprehend desperate thieves and murderers, and to put my very life at risk more than once. But never had he made such an utterly bizarre request.

"Good lord, Holmes," I sputtered and again demanded, "Have you gone stark raving mad?"

"Why of course, I have," he replied, still smiling. "Is not that what falling in love is all about."

For the next several minutes, I argued with him. But he was adamant. He would not budge from his request, indeed his demand, that I not only write a letter to his red-headed vixen but that I write it as coming from me and sign it. He was relentless, and I eventually gave in.

"Ah Watson, how can I thank you? If it succeeds, I assure you I will die a happy man."

I bit my tongue and refrained from the rejoinder that it was debatable he might die happy, but it was certain that he would die poorer. I took out a pen and paper and, with significant dictating from Holmes, wrote a letter from Dr. John H. Watson to the admittedly beautiful Miss Ruth Lightowlers, attempting to convince her that Sherlock Holmes was not only in love with her but wanted to marry her.

"Now then," said Holmes, "conclude by begging her to come to the Corpus Christi Church in Maiden Lane at 11:00 on Friday morning, if she wishes to become Mrs. Sherlock Holmes. You might also note that you will be standing up for me as my best man."

I wrote as he had demanded even though in both my head and my heart, I considered the entire venture utter nonsense. When I had finished the final draft on a crisp, clean piece of notepaper, I handed it to Holmes. He read it in its entirety, smiled, and inserted the note into an envelope.

"And would you mind," he asked, "writing out the address as given in her note to me?" I did, and he quickly sealed the envelope, pulled on his coat and was out the door, envelope in hand.

All I could do was to pray that Providence would intervene and that Holmes would come to his senses.

Although, I had to admit that I had never seen him smile so genuinely as when he rhapsodized over his red-head.

Chapter Eleven
A Marriage Not Made in
Heaven

Providence did not intervene.

On Friday morning, I reluctantly put on my formal morning suit, polished shoes, spats, and a well-brushed hat and trudged slowly down the steps to Baker Street. Holmes was in front of me, similarly attired, and seemed to be walking with a spring in his step.

"What if she does not appear?" I asked.

"Oh, I think that unlikely. I fully expect that she shall arrive at the appointed hour and that the two of us shall meet the blushing bride at the steps of the church. By noon hour, I shall be a married man."

We reached the church at twenty minutes before eleven o'clock and entered. The organist was seated and practicing his processional, while an older stooped man was busy polishing the brass on the altar.

"Where is the priest?" I asked Holmes.

"Oh, do not worry," Holmes replied. "Father McSweeney assured me that he would be here at just before eleven o'clock. He was quite pleased that I asked him to officiate. It seems that he has been a faithful reader of your sensational stories about me for many years."

I walked back toward the door of the church. A small table had been set up in the narthex, and a marriage register book lay open on it. Seated behind the table was a fellow in a cassock who, I assumed, must be the registrar of births, deaths, marriages, and goodness only knows what all else. We went outside and stood on the steps in the cold, waiting for the bride to appear.

At two minutes before eleven o'clock, a well-polished carriage pulled up and out of it stepped a woman who, I had to admit, was beyond stunning in her beauty. She was not wearing a bridal gown but was attired in a very stylish ivory-colored dress that augmented the translucence of her pale skin and rich auburn hair. Her smile was radiant.

"I was prepared," she said, "to arrive and find no groom, but here you are." She laughed merrily, walked up to Holmes and kissed him on the cheek. Holmes gave her his arm and led her into the church. In the narthex, he stopped and turned back to me.

"My dear Watson, would you mind taking a moment with Father McSweeney about matters related to the signing of the registrar and then meet us at the altar?"

At the registrar's table stood a small man, wearing a priest's vestments, and chatting with the registrar as he leaned over the table. He was not facing me, but I could see that he was somewhat elderly, with long gray hair, and a large set of spectacles propped up on his nose.

"Father McSweeney," I said, "I am Doctor John Watson. I will be serving as witness to the wedding and standing up for Sherlock Holmes."

I felt a hand suddenly grasp my arm near the elbow and forcefully pull me over until my head was almost touching that of the priest.

"Watson, do not make a sound," was whispered in my ear.

I looked at the priest and nearly fainted. Behind the eyeglasses and under the wig of hair, was the sallow, ferret face of Inspector Lestrade.

"Follow me up the aisle," he said in my ear. "Then stand behind Holmes and keep silent."

He turned and began to hobble slowly up the aisle, through the nave, and up to the altar. I was beyond speechless, but somehow pulled my wits together and followed him.

Holmes and the woman who I now seriously doubted was about to become Mrs. Sherlock Holmes were standing in front of the altar, gazing lovingly into each other's eyes. The priest came around and stood in front of them.

"Do you have the ring?" he asked Holmes in a low and shaking voice.

"I do," said Holmes.

"Good. Let me see it. We must take a second to practice. I do so not like it when the groom has bought one that is too small and will have to push it onto a bride's chubby finger. It is quite distressing. So, here now. Let me ascertain that it will fit before we get the service underway. My dear young lady, kindly give me your left hand."

The bride graciously extended her hand to the priest. He quickly grasped it with his left hand and in one sudden move snapped a handcuff onto her extended wrist.

"Miss Bernadette O'Donohue, I am placing you under arrest. You are charged with the aiding and abetting in the murder of Professor Hume-Craw, with the murder of Miss Rowena Ferguson, with the murder of Mr. Lloyd Sunday, and with the theft of archeological treasure that belongs to the British Museum. I advise you that anything you say can and will be used against you at trial."

For a brief moment, nothing happened. Then the woman turned and made as if to run away. Unfortunately for her, the other end of the handcuffs was affixed firmly to the wrist of Inspector Lestrade, and she was yanked back. In one swift move, she thrust her hand into a fold in her dress and out came a small revolver. She pointed it directly at the chest of Lestrade.

"Undo the lock immediately," she said, "or I swear I will kill you and Sherlock Holmes."

"Pardon me, Miss" came a voice from the side of the nave. "But you need to drop that gun or else I will have to fire on you. It would be a crying shame to ruin not only a lovely dress but one of the finest posteriors in all of London."

The chap who had been polishing the altar was now standing a few yards away. He was holding a rifle and had it pointed directly at Bernadette O'Donohue.

"That would go double for me, Miss. Best drop the gun." This command came from the organist, who was likewise pointing a rifle at the bride. The fellow who had been sitting at the registrar table was now walking up the aisle toward us, and also holding a rifle that was pointed directly at her.

Earlier in this story, I noted that the warm gaze of this woman would have melted the frost off the window. Now, the blazing heat from her eyes might have melted the window itself. She turned her face toward Holmes and uttered several words which propriety does not permit me to record here. She dropped the revolver on the floor, took a breath, and in a composed voice spoke.

"I fear you have all made a foolish mistake. I demand to be taken immediately to my solicitor in the Inner Temple. I will not respond to any questions until he is present."

Holmes nodded at her and walked back down the aisle, giving me a tug on the arm as he passed.

"Come, Watson. The game is over. It is time to celebrate victory. Simpson's in the Strand is only a block away. They serve an excellent luncheon."

He was already walking quickly out of the church. I scrambled to keep up with him as we walked a few steps along Maiden Lane and turned on to Southampton Street. He had assumed the posture and carriage that I had seen so often in the past when he was satisfied that he had completed his case.

I, however, was furious.

"Holmes," I snapped as we were seated at a table. "You deceived me. You lied to me. You made a fool of me."

I would have gone on in unrestrained anger had he not interrupted me.

"Oh, Watson, Watson. My dear friend. Of course, I deceived you. I had no choice. I could not have possibly done what I did without your help. You were magnificent."

"What do you mean, magnificent? I was played for a dupe."

"And you played your role perfectly, my dear man. I may have some skills in acting and playing the part of a decrepit bookseller, but I have never before been assigned the role of a man in love. Pretending to be such was far beyond my abilities. Bernadette O'Donohue is one of the wiliest women I have ever met. I was certain that she would see through my pretense, and I dare say she did. It was only when you met with her and so sincerely told her of my hopeless attraction to her and my desire to marry her that she was convinced. Her arrest is mostly to your credit."

I was not in the least appeased and was about to launch into a tirade when Inspector Lestrade joined us at the table. He had managed to lose his vestments and wig.

"Ah, Father McSweeney," said Holmes. "How good of you to join us. Have you sent the villainess off under guard?"

"She has one arm handcuffed to Gregson and the other to Bradstreet. She is not going anywhere."

"An excellent precaution. She is as crafty as Odysseus and as ruthless as Atilla. Do not give her an inch, or she will take a mile before you know it."

Inspector Lestrade now turned to me and reached out his arm and gave me a firm pat on the back.

"Dr. Watson. Well done, sir. Holmes tells me that you were the genius behind trapping this daughter of Jezebel. It was your meeting with her and your letter that did the trick and brought her back. Without you, she would likely be in Vienna by now. Well done, sir."

I feigned a humble reply, and Lestrade turned back to Holmes. He lifted his glass of wine and spoke to Holmes.

"Enough of my thanking the two of you. Now, out with it, Holmes. How is heaven's name did you put all the pieces together."

"Ah, where to begin?" said Holmes as he lit another cigarette.

"Begin at the beginning," I said, very wearily, "and go on till you come to the end: then stop."

Holmes smiled a warm smile and began.

"It began when the woman first walked into 221B Baker Street. Why even you, my dear Watson, spotted the incongruity of her expensive boots and perfume with her deliberately inexpensive dress and coat. However, the first thing you failed to notice was the redness of her eyes."

I objected. "Not true Holmes. I could see that she had recently been crying."

"Oh, my good man. She had been doing nothing of the sort. She used a common theatrical trick and held a lit cigarette under her eyes before entering. It brings redness to the eyes without so much as altering the least little spot of her perfectly applied cosmetics. There was a faint odor of tobacco to her which she had attempted to mask with a fresh application of the perfume. Add to that the evidence of her hands and wrists."

"I looked there as well," I said. "She did not have the lines across her wrists that you have made a point of observing in the past. What was there to see?"

"Please, my friend. Just like the dog that did not bark, it was the absence, not the presence that was of singular interest. She claimed to have been working as a private secretary. Had that been true, the telltale marks of a typist would have been present. Therefore, I took her right hand into mine so that I could observe it more closely. Two things stood out. There was a distinct callous on the pad of her index finger, and the backs of her hands were darker than the skin on her arm in the area normally covered by a sleeve. That informed me that she was a skilled and experienced telegraph operator who had quite recently acquired a suntan. You yourself noticed the skin on the back of her neck, which, when taken into consideration along with her hand and wrist, was a conclusive indication of having returned recently from someplace sunny and warm. France, at this time of year, is neither.

"Her claim of having been raised in poverty with a mother who takes in laundry was a preposterous falsehood brazenly designed to arouse my pity and admiration. Whether we like it or not, class cannot be disguised. A woman who moves and acts with her grace and confidence did not grow up in a poor family from Connemara. Her trace accent was undoubtedly Irish, as was her appearance, but she obviously came from a family that was not without means and had paid for a respectable education."

"But Holmes," I said, "she thoroughly convinced you at first. When did you know that she was attempting to trick you?"

"She did no such thing. When you know immediately that someone is trying to deceive you, the most unproductive response is to the expose the deception straight away. Doing so means that you learn nothing. What you must do is play along and trick that person into believing that he or she has succeeded in tricking you. Obviously, her intent was to have me not only believe her story but to engender my sympathy and indeed my affection. Therefore, I gave her both in spades. Now, I confess, that I knew that I was utterly lacking in the skills of portraying a man falling in love, which is why I would have to depend on you, my dear doctor, to give a rave review of my inadequate performance. And you, being the soul of honesty, could not have done that convincingly if you yourself did not believe it. It was you who turned me into a believable lover."

"Right," interjected Lestrade. "Enough of your playing Romeo. How did you come to know that she was a cold-hearted killer?"

"Ah, that took some time. Even I hesitated to consider the possibility that an attractive young woman could be a cold-blooded murderer. However, I had to start with the question of who could have tossed the professor overboard. Miss O'Donohue is simply not physically capable of doing that on her own. One of the students could have, but we eliminated them as suspects. His daughter, the one who is built like a scrum-half, could have done it with one arm, but that would require a conclusion of patricide, which demands a motive far beyond mere greed for treasure. It was possible that the officials from the Museum, avaricious as they are for glory to their institution, might have hired a local killer and arranged the theft, but there would have been no reason for doing so. The treasure was destined to come to them anyway. Their competition in Crete from the Arthur Evans expedition did not need to find more ancient treasure. They already had enough of their own.

"For a while, all of the fingers appeared to point at Mr. Lloyd Sunday, possibly acting in cooperation with Miss O'Donohue. We knew that the only two people who had directly seen and understood the value of the treasure were the professor and Mr. Sunday. The others had only been told and had seen Sunday's drawing of it. Given that Miss

O'Donohue had already revealed her willingness to use her beauty and her wiles to have men do her bidding, I theorized that, at some time after seeing the drawing, she had decided to seduce Sunday, become his paramour, and convince him to join her in getting rid of the professor and stealing the statue. Or perhaps it was Sunday who initiated the scheme. Who played the lead in the deadly duo we will never know, but they appear to have acted in concert up until the time when Sunday was murdered by a ruthless woman who decided to keep the entire treasure for herself."

"Holmes," said Lestrade, "that seems somewhat incongruous. If this woman is as clever as she appears to have been, why would she put herself at such a great risk by murdering her accomplice? And do so in broad daylight where she could have easily been spotted and apprehended?"

"An excellent question," said Holmes. "You are quite correct. It does not appear to be a logical action by an exceptionally conniving woman. All I can offer as an answer at the moment is to note that she is Irish, a redhead, and a female. Consistent logic is not the strong suit of such a group of people, but I admit that such a response is not entirely satisfactory."

"Yes," agreed Lestrade. "And if the order of events you have presented is correct, then this woman was so cold-blooded that she could murder her accomplice, jimmy the locker and steal the statue, and an hour later cheerily prance into her lunch with Dr. Watson as if nothing had happened."

I was beyond horrified. To think that I had sat across from her over an elegant lunch whilst the blood on her hands was only a few hours old. How Holmes had concluded that she did, in fact, shoot Lloyd Sunday was not clear, and I asked him about it.

"Oh, Watson, again, I could not have done it without you. Your sincere protestations to her of my honorable intentions led directly to my being invited into her private chambers in Clerkenwell. She did not live in a rented room in a go-down on Wamer Street but in a quite respectable terrace house. Immediately upon departing from it, I went directly to the city clerk's office to look into the ownership. It was registered to a Bernadette O'Donohue. At that point, her true identity was revealed.

"Whilst I was in her rooms," Holmes continued, "I observed an ashtray in which there was a small pile of residue from a cigarette. I examined it quickly with my glass and determined that it had come from a Tabby's Navy Cut, the same brand that we later found in Sunday's room. Without my assistance, she had managed on her own to track him down. Add to that the evidence of how he was shot. If someone were approaching you with a gun, would you stand still, unbutton your overcoat, and then your suit jacket and allow him to place a gun against your sternum? Of course, you would not. You might struggle, or you might turn and flee, but you would never stand still and allow yourself to be murdered. But that is precisely how Sunday had reacted. It was at point-blank range with a gun held against his chest. The reddish mark on his cheek beside his mouth was the additional clue. It was not a bruise; it was lipstick. A woman had approached him and he, for reasons of sensuality, had opened his coat and suit jacket to enhance the romantic pleasure. She engaged him in an amorous embrace, placed a kiss on his cheek, and pulled the trigger. Had he been shot by a man, the evidence would have been otherwise. It was conclusive that he was shot by a woman at very close range and there was only one woman who could have and would have done that."

"But what about the poor young woman, Miss Rowena?" asked Lestrade. "Did not Sunday murder her? But then you told me to charge O'Donohue with that murder as well."

"Of course, I did. My instincts at first were to draw the same conclusion as you as the true nature of what took place was beyond horrifying. But reason prevailed. It was obvious from the evidence that the unfortunate Miss Rowena, for whose death I cannot entirely absolve myself, was killed by another woman. Even you, my dear Inspector, assumed that such a modest and circumspect woman would never have a man present in her flat whilst she sat in her underwear at her dressing table. Your conclusion that a man must have entered through the window and surprised her had to be ruled out. Why? Because she was sitting in front of a large mirror. She would have seen someone approaching from behind and would not have sat still whilst he cut her throat. There was no sign of any struggle. The items on the table were undisturbed. The hairbrush was sitting on the coffee table. The only explanation that made sense was that another woman, a known friend, had been standing behind her, affectionately brushing her hair and whilst doing so had extracted a knife or razor from her pocket and cut the poor young thing's throat."

"But why?" I demanded. "There was no reason."

"*Au contraire, mon ami,*" said Holmes. "Miss O'Donohue was part of the same clutch of young woman telegraph operators who worked together in the Mount Pleasant Royal Mail center. They were friends. Do you not recall Miss Rowena referring to one of the members of the group as Bernie? She quit her position at the same time as the demands for the contents of telegraphed material that could be used for blackmail ceased. The demands returned after O'Donohue returned to London from Crete."

"No," I objected. "If O'Donohue was one of the victims of the blackguard calling himself Charles Augustus Milverton, then Bernie should have cut his throat, not Rowena's."

"Not at all," replied Holmes. "There was no blackguard calling himself Charles Augustus Milverton. *She* was Charles Augustus Milverton. It was highly unlikely that a man, unknown to any of the women working for the Royal Mail, could amass such closely guarded secrets of seven young women. But, as your wives will confirm to you, it is entirely normal behavior amongst women to divulge their life histories, including their scandalous secrets to other women, even those who are near strangers that they meet in a lavatory. It is one of the greatest strengths and terrible weaknesses of the fair sex. They trust each other. Rowena, Eleanor, and the others had unsuspectingly disclosed their secrets to each other, including Bernadette O'Donohue, and she took advantage of the opportunity."

"Acting alone?" demanded Lestrade. "You know my thoughts on groups of criminals. There is always someone pulling the strings. That's even more likely when the gang are all women."

"I assure you, Inspector that you underestimate the fair sex, but, I confess, you could quite possibly be right. I submit to you that both of us may have more work to do."

"And why did she leave and go off on a scholarly dig?"

"An excellent question," replied Holmes. "As to why she decided to leave her lucrative scheme at the Royal Mail, I can only guess. She would have come across information about the Evans expeditions and the one planned by Professor Hume-Craw. It is possible that she expected some treasure to be unearthed that could bring additional riches to her. Or, it may be that she had tired of the miserable fall weather and elected to spend her days in Mediterranean climes. It is safe to assume that she used her seductive charms on the professor, who had a history of being prone to such temptations, and she joined the expedition."

To this, I added my observation. "The man's tendency to think with his little head when he should have used his big head has had rather unfortunate consequences."

To which Lestrade said, "It always does."

The inspector now pushed his chair back from the table, leaned back and crossed his arms over his chest. "Holmes," he said, "again I must congratulate you. Everything you have said makes complete sense. By all rights, this woman should be hanged for her crimes, but I fear that may present a problem."

"Good lord," I said, "why would you say that? She is as deserving of the gallows as anyone I have ever heard of."

"Right you are, doctor," said Lestrade. "But there are no witnesses. Had Sunday still been alive, I might have been able to have the two of them turn and testify against each other. But that opportunity went down the river with Sunday."

"What of the other women," I asked, "who worked in the telegraph unit with O'Donohue? Could they be of assistance?"

Lestrade pondered that suggestion for a moment. "Not likely. Not one of them appears to have suspected anything, and the only one willing to take a risk ended up with her throat cut. Proving the crime of tampering with the mail would be enough to send her away for several years, but where is the evidence? And would those other young women be willing to now have their secrets exposed when they are no longer being forced to aid blackmail? I fear that would be unlikely."

"Then we must," said Holmes, "leave it to you and the Crown to put together the best case you can. And while you are at it, you might try to locate the golden statue. I fear that our shrewd Miss O'Donohue is the only one left who knows its whereabouts. And I suspect that she is not about to divulge that knowledge."

"Might she have been willing to share it with her husband?" I asked.

Holmes laughed at the suggestions. "I confess that I have no idea and that we shall never know. Regardless of her barrage of compliments concerning my mind, my character, and even my physique, there is no doubt she showed up at the church—thanks to your wonderfully effective missive—because she had concluded that being married to Sherlock Holmes would result in my expending my talents to protect her, as any faithful husband should be expected to do."

"Not a role," said Lestrade, "that I imagine for you anytime in the next fifty years."

Chapter Twelve
Miss Charlotte Europa
Golderton

During the next two weeks, the Press was full of the story. Having a scandalous account of a merciless killer who was also a stunningly beautiful woman was a gift to them from whatever gods they worshipped. Most of the papers wallowed in the lurid details, augmented by creative speculation as to how this Irish beauty had seduced not only the men she murdered but possibly even the poor Miss Rowena. Miss O'Donohue's capacities for evil were portrayed as bordering on supernatural, leading several of the more popular papers to speculate that she must be in league with Beelzebub.

The woman herself continued to proclaim her innocence and put the blame directly on the competition from the Ashmolean expedition and even on the person of Arthur Evans.

To my surprise, a few of the papers seemed to be sympathetic to her and endlessly stressed the circumstantial nature of the evidence and the unrelenting competition between not only the leading British museums but also amongst the great institutions all across Europe and America. That the entire affair could have been masterminded by the Russians or, more likely, some American interests, was a plausible alternative, they insisted.

It occurred to me, perhaps unfairly but I suspect not, that some reporters and editors might have been careless in the contents of their telegrams and were now paying the price to avoid their sins becoming known. It was far from impossible that they might have received a message advising them of their perilous position should they not portray Miss Bernadette O'Donohue in a kindly light.

My dear wife had returned to our home, and I was no longer seeing Sherlock Holmes every morning and evening. My curiosity, however, got the better of me and one afternoon in early February, with the hours of sunlight now being somewhat longer than they had been in January, I strolled over to 221B Baker Street after finishing my appointments with my patients.

Holmes was sitting in his usual armchair, puffing on his pipe, and reading a file. He gestured to me to help myself to the brandy on the mantle and be seated. I did both.

"Holmes," I said, "now put down the pipe and whatever it is you are reading and enlighten me. What has become of the beautiful killer that was prepared to marry you?"

He laid down his pipe, and a look of resignation swept over his face.

"One must never," he said, "underestimate the ability of a brilliant woman when she is desperate. She had another card up her sleeve that she has now played."

"Yes, go on."

"The British Museum."

"What of it?"

"They want that statue, and she is the only one who knows where it is. She has let them know that she will never reveal the location if she is sent to the gallows, and will not divulge whilst she remains in prison. As a result, the Museum has hired the best lawyers and is letting it be known amongst their stable of press reporters, that our lady should get off with not much more than a slap on the wrist."

"That would be an unspeakable travesty," I said. "She should hang."

"Indeed, she should, but Lestrade has informed me that given the weak circumstantial evidence for the murders, they are moving ahead only with the charge of threatening a police

155

officer with a firearm. It is expected that she will plead guilty to that charge and serve a year, two at the most, in prison."

"Is there nothing you can do about it?" I asked.

He did not immediately answer, as he sat there pondering. Whatever his answer might have been, I will never know, for we were interrupted by a knock on the door.

Mrs. Hudson soon appeared bearing two cards.

"There are two women to see you, Mr. Holmes. The one you have seen before, the scrum-half. She's carrying a small steamer trunk. The other could be her mother."

The first card was indeed from Miss Gertrude Hume-Craw. The other read:

Margaret Hume-Craw (Mrs.)
27A Thistle Lane
St. Andrews, Scotland

The two women entered the room. The younger one deposited the trunk rather forcefully on our coffee table. The older woman was as tall as the younger, but nowhere near as physically imposing. She was finely attired and had an attractive mature face, topped by neatly arranged gray hair.

"Holmes, Watson, meet my mother," said Gertrude Hume-Craw. "This is not the mother I asked you to find."

"A pleasure to meet you," said Holmes. He was looking at her with one eye and eyeing the trunk with the other.

"And it is an honor to meet you, Mr. Holmes, and you as well Dr. Watson," said the older lady. "I regret I did not agree to meet you when you came to St. Andrews. Please forgive my daughter's lack of manners. Her lack of any social graces is a constant source of embarrassment to me."

"Mum, put a sock in it. In case you two blokes cannot discern something, let me enlighten you. My mother and I do not get along. She despises me, and I return the favor. But the death of dear old daddy has forced us to join forces if we ever want to get anything from the estate. So here we are, working together, at least for now."

"And would you be so kind as to explain the reason for your visit?" asked Holmes.

Miss Gertrude was about to speak, but her mother answered first.

"We apologize for coming without an appointment. I had thought that my daughter would have had the manners to request one in advance, but that did not happen. Our reason for coming is, as she has said, tied to the estate of my recently departed husband. The British Museum has, through its select group of lawyers, put a freeze on the distribution of any of the assets of my husband's estate until the matter of the missing statue is resolved."

"That could take years, "I said. "Unless you can get that injunction lifted, it will be a long time before Miss O'Donohue is willing to reveal its location and have the cloud on your inheritance lifted."

"Fortunately," replied Mrs. Hume-Craw, "that may not be necessary. My reason for optimism lies in this trunk."

"Madam," said Holmes, "kindly explain. Who or what is in the trunk?"

"Charlotte."

"Are you referring to the Minoan statue?"

"No, Mr. Holmes," said the younger woman. "She is referring to the barmaid down at the corner. Of course, she is referring to the missing statue. Do you know any other Charlotte that would bring us to see you?"

"Again, Mr. Holmes," said Mrs. Hume-Craw, "please excuse my daughter's belligerence. Yes, we are speaking of the statue. If you will open the trunk, you will see what I mean."

I stood up and moved to a place where I could open the latches of the trunk. Inside was a layer of packing straw through which I carefully threaded my fingers until they touched something hard and solid. Slowly, I lifted an object about eighteen inches in height and perhaps a foot across. It was wrapped in several layers of cloth and was not particularly heavy.

"Careful, doc," said Gertrude, "She's breakable."

Whatever it was that I was lifting was obviously not a gold statue, as such are not at all breakable but exceptionally heavy.

Whilst I held the mysterious object in the air, Holmes lifted the trunk out of the way, allowing me to set the object on the table. Slowly, I removed the strips of wool blanket that were wrapped around it. What emerged was beyond belief.

"Is this your idea of a joke?" I said. "If it is, then it is in extremely poor taste."

The object in front of me was indeed a statue of sorts. It was made of pottery and painted in gaudy colors. And it was utterly, disgustingly obscene. On top of a base of about a foot square, there was a figure of a white bull, standing on its haunches. The face was painted as a lewd caricature, a bull with his leering eyes bulging and his red tongue sticking out. The other figure was of a buxom woman whose face had been altered to look somewhat bovine, and given a look of demented ecstasy. Her posterior region was impaled on the bull's male appendage. On the base was written an obscene limerick. On one side it was written in English, on the other sides, a crude translation of the limerick in French, Spanish, and Italian.

"Madam," I said sharply. "bringing such a vulgar object into this home and presenting to two gentlemen is highly offensive. What do you think you are doing?"

I admit that I was angry. The thing in front of me was of the sort that could be found for sale in the cheapest East End brothel.

The woman smiled at me and then laughed. "My feelings exactly, Dr. Watson. It is precisely how I reacted when my dear departed and not particularly lamented husband brought it home one day. As you have likely learned by now, he had a weakness for all things related to indulging the pleasures of the flesh, whether they be porcelain souvenir objects, dime novels—he was a subscriber to *The Pearl*—or voluptuous young secretaries. He collected them all, and when tired of his latest acquisition, he would move on to the next. One day he returned to St. Andrews from Blackpool and proudly displayed this god-awful monstrosity you see in front of you. He called it *Charlotte Europa* and insisted on having it in our bedroom. It sat on his dresser for a few weeks until he took his next trip abroad, whereupon I wrapped the horrid thing up, stuck in in this trunk and put it in the basement and out of sight. When he returned, he brought with him another one of his artistic treasures which, not being nearly as vulgar, was placed on his dresser. Charlotte Europa was gone from his mind. It has been in my basement for these past fifteen years, utterly forgotten. That is until recently.

"I read in the papers the story of my husband's disappearance, and then of the arrest of his latest mistress for his murder along with those of Lloyd Sunday and the poor young mother from Ayr. At first, I merely shrugged my shoulders and was not at all surprised. Edgar always played too close to the law and had been challenged on numerous occasions for plagiarism in his published articles and for demanding ungentlemanly favors of the secretaries. But then came the description of the so-called priceless statue that had been stolen. I read it, and I exclaimed, 'Why that's Charlotte. She's in my basement.' I knew immediately that he had fabricated the entire story of the discovery of the statue. He made it up. There never was any statue. But he could not come back to the Museum empty-handed, so he concocted the story, had Lloyd Sunday draw a picture of it, using his memory of Charlotte Europa as a guide, and then he would, no doubt, have arranged to have the priceless artifact stolen before it could be turned over to the greedy old chaps at the museum."

"But why then would she murder Sunday?" I asked.

"For that, sir," Mrs. Hume-Craw said, "I have no explanation."

"Well I do," said her daughter. "And you do not have to be Sherlock Holmes to figure it out. Want to hear it, doc?"

"Please, but do try to refrain from vulgarity."

"Always," she said. "Well, it happened like this. The whole expedition was a disaster. Evans and his gang had cornered the only site worth digging up, and all we came up with was junk. So, daddy and Lloyd come up with the idea of the greatest find ever and, like mum said, it had to get stolen. Dad and Lloyd are the only ones who know the truth. They tell all the rest of us the story, show us the drawing, and we believe them. But daddy doesn't know that the mistress he hired for the expedition is ruthless. She goes to Lloyd and tries to use her seductive charms on him. She says that the two of them should get rid of the professor, steal the statue, and then hold it for ransom and split the proceeds. She tries to persuade Lloyd by agreeing to become his mistress as well. She thinks that Lloyd is a dupe, but he's not. He's a cad, and a smart one. He knows that there is no statue, but he has this gorgeous young harlot offering to keep him company late in the evenings. He might be getting sloppy seconds, but it's fun all the same. So, he agrees, and together they toss daddy overboard, and when they get to Marseilles, Lloyd tells her that he has sneaked the statue off the boat and sent it overland to London. She says she'll continue to be his mistress after they get to London but he doesn't show up with the statue. She tracks him down then Lloyd laughs at Bernadette and tells her that he played her for a fool and thank you very much and good-bye. And that if she tries to do anything about it, he will go to the police and confess and she'll swing. Well, Lloyd thinks the sweet, Irish, redhead is going to have a bit of a temper tantrum and then a little cry and a sulk and go away. He's wrong. Like the man said, hell hath no fury like a woman scorned. She's madder than a hornet and pretends to give him a kiss good-bye and shoots him. Then she pushes his body into the river, but she thinks that maybe he was lying about the statue and it really is in the locker. But she forgets to get the key, and the body is now floating away. So, she finds a jimmy and goes back to the locker and forces it and find nothing.

"So that's my theory, Mr. Sherlock Holmes. If you can come up with a better one, let me know. Otherwise, since you agreed to have me as your client, I'm instructing you to take Charlotte to the blokes at the Museum and let them know they were duped and get them to take off the injunction on the estate, and then you get paid. What do you think of that offer, Mr. Sherlock Holmes."

I could sense that Holmes was seething with anger as he sat and looked at the daughter for a long time without speaking. Finally, he answered.

"I believe it would be good for both of you to depart. I will be in contact with you within two days to advise you of the resolution of your case."

"That will do for me," she said. "Careful you don't drop Charlotte."

The younger woman exited the room, leaving her mother behind.

"Mr. Holmes," she began.

Please," he interrupted. "No further words are necessary. You have put up with enough in your life. For your sake, I will see that the matters are resolved. And permit me to bring to your attention that you are now a widow and free to enjoy such remaining years are you are granted on this earth. I wish you well."

She smiled and departed. Sherlock Holmes sat back in his chair, lit a cigarette, and gazed into the fire.

"Watson," he said. "when you come to write up your account of this case, it would be accurate to note that I, Sherlock Holmes, acknowledge, that it was not one that left me with any sense of satisfaction."

"But you did solve the case. The mystery has been resolved."

"Has it? Or is the puppet master still at large?"

For the next several minutes, Holmes continued with his smoking and gazing into the flames whilst I sipped on a brandy. My admiration for his dedication to his calling was as strong as ever but I had to admit that I was still smarting from his deceiving me. I could not resist one last suggestion.

"Of course," I casually added, "if you really do find yourself feeling lonely and wishing for the comfort of loving female companionship, my wife has several still attractive, highly educated friends of a certain age who would be delighted to become Mrs. Sherlock Holmes."

"Watson, that prospect is utterly horrifying."

A request to all readers:

After reading this story, please help the author and future readers by taking a moment to write a short, constructive review on the site from which you purchased the book. Thank you.   CSC

Dear Sherlockian Readers:

In this story, I have attempted to pay tribute not only to the original Sherlock Holmes story, but also to the great mystery story tradition of the *femme fatale*. Mystery lovers will note the obvious borrowing from Dashiell Hammett's masterpiece, *The Maltese Falcon*.

As the island of Malta had already been taken, I just moved along the water a little to Crete (I had learned about it in high school history class), and went from there.

The Minoan Civilization took place on the island of Crete from about 2000 to 1500 BC. It was first investigated by the British scholar and archeologist (and former director of the Ashmolean Museum), Arthur Evans between 1901 and 1905. Within the ruins of the great palace of Knossos in present-day Heraklion, he discovered the maze that he claimed was The Labyrinth of the mythical Minotaur, and numerous clay tablets that were inscribed with two unknown languages that he named 'Linear A' and 'Linear B.'

Linear B was finally deciphered in the 1950s by Michael Ventris, using code-breaking techniques developed during World War II. Liner A remains undeciphered. The references to the exceptional work of Arthur Evans in the story are generally accurate and the snide comments from his fictional competition, the Hume-Craw Expedition, should be mostly ignored.

The related stories of Zeus's becoming a bull and raping Europa, and of Parsiphaë and her offspring, the Minotaur, can be found in any adult collection of Greek mythology.

The local geography of London is accurate for the time setting. The Rusack Hotel still stands at the edge of The Old Course in St. Andrews and continues to be beloved by the golf aficionados of the world.

The officers of the British Museum named in the story held the positions ascribed to them in 1901 but were, no doubt, far finer gentlemen than I have unfairly portrayed them.

Thank you reading this New Sherlock Holmes Mystery. Hope you enjoyed it.

Warm regards,

Craig

A request to all readers:

After reading this story, please help the author and future readers by taking a moment to write a short, constructive review on the site from which you purchased the book. Thank you.   CSC

About the Author

In May of 2014 the Sherlock Holmes Society of Canada – better known as The Bootmakers – announced a contest for a new Sherlock Holmes story. Although he had no experience writing fiction, the author submitted a short Sherlock Holmes mystery and was blessed to be declared one of the winners. Thus inspired, he has continued to write new Sherlock Holmes Mysteries since and is on a mission to write a new story as a tribute to each of the sixty stories in the original Canon. He currently writes from Toronto, the Okanagan, and Manhattan. Several readers of New Sherlock Holmes Mysteries have kindly sent him suggestions for future stories. You are welcome to do likewise at craigstephencopland@gmail.com.

More Historical Mysteries
by Craig Stephen Copland
www.SherlockHolmesMystery.com

Copy the links to look inside and download

Studying Scarlet. Starlet O'Halloran, a fabulous mature woman, who reminds the reader of Scarlet O'Hara (but who, for copyright reasons cannot actually be her) has arrived in London looking for her long-lost husband, Brett (who resembles Rhett Butler, but who, for copyright reasons, cannot actually be him). She enlists the help of Sherlock Holmes. This is an unauthorized parody, inspired by Arthur Conan Doyle's *A Study in Scarlet* and Margaret Mitchell's *Gone with the Wind*. http://authl.it/aic

The Sign of the Third*.* Fifteen hundred years ago the courageous Princess Hemamali smuggled the sacred tooth of the Buddha into Ceylon. Now, for the first time, it is being brought to London to be part of a magnificent exhibit at the British Museum. But what if something were to happen to it? It would be a disaster for the British Empire. Sherlock Holmes, Dr. Watson, and even Mycroft Holmes are called upon to prevent such a crisis. This novella is inspired by the Sherlock Holmes mystery, *The Sign of the Four*. http://authl.it/aie

A Sandal from East Anglia. Archeological excavations at an old abbey unearth an ancient document that has the potential to change the course of the British Empire and all of Christendom. Holmes encounters some evil young men and a strikingly beautiful young Sister, with a curious double life. The mystery is inspired by the original Sherlock Holmes story, *A Scandal in Bohemia.* http://authl.it/aif

The Bald-Headed Trust. Watson insists on taking Sherlock Holmes on a short vacation to the seaside in Plymouth. No sooner has Holmes arrived than he is needed to solve a double murder and prevent a massive fraud diabolically designed by the evil Professor himself. Who knew that a family of devout conservative churchgoers could come to the aid of Sherlock Holmes and bring enormous grief to evil doers? The story is inspired by *The Red-Headed League.* http://authl.it/aih

A Case of Identity Theft. It is the fall of 1888 and Jack the Ripper is terrorizing London. A young married couple is found, minus their heads. Sherlock Holmes, Dr. Watson, the couple's mothers, and Mycroft must join forces to find the murderer before he kills again and makes off with half a million pounds. The novella is a tribute to *A Case of Identity.* It will appeal both to devoted fans of Sherlock Holmes, as well as to those who love the great game of rugby. http://authl.it/aii

The Hudson Valley Mystery. A young man in New York went mad and murdered his father. His mother believes he is innocent and knows he is not crazy. She appeals to Sherlock Holmes and, together with Dr. and Mrs. Watson, he crosses the Atlantic to help this client in need. This new story was inspired by *The Boscombe Valley Mystery.* http://authl.it/aij

The Mystery of the Five Oranges. A desperate father enters 221B Baker Street. His daughter has been kidnapped and spirited off to North America. The evil network who have taken her has spies everywhere. There is only one hope – Sherlock Holmes. Sherlockians will enjoy this new adventure, inspired by *The Five Orange Pips* and *Anne of Green Gables* http://authl.it/aik

. www.SherlockHolmesMystery.com

The Man Who Was Twisted But Hip. France is torn apart by The Dreyfus Affair. Westminster needs Sherlock Holmes so that the evil tide of anti-Semitism that has engulfed France will not spread. Sherlock and Watson go to Paris to solve the mystery and thwart Moriarty. This new mystery is inspired by, *The Man with the Twisted Lip,* as well as by *The Hunchback of Notre Dame.* http://authl.it/ail

The Adventure of the Blue Belt Buckle. A young street urchin discovers a man's belt and buckle under a bush in Hyde Park. A body is found in a hotel room in Mayfair. Scotland Yard seeks the help of Sherlock Holmes in solving the murder. The Queen's Jubilee could be ruined. Sherlock Holmes, Dr. Watson, Scotland Yard, and Her Majesty all team up to prevent a crime of unspeakable dimensions. A new mystery inspired by *The Blue Carbuncle.* http://authl.it/aim

The Adventure of the Spectred Bat. A beautiful young woman, just weeks away from giving birth, arrives at Baker Street in the middle of the night. Her sister was attacked by a bat and died, and now it is attacking her. A vampire? The story is a tribute to *The Adventure of the Speckled Band* and like the original, leaves the mind wondering and the heart racing. http://authl.it/ain

The Adventure of the Engineer's Mom. A brilliant young Cambridge University engineer is carrying out secret research for the Admiralty. It will lead to the building of the world's most powerful battleship, The Dreadnaught. His adventuress mother is kidnapped, and he seeks the help of Sherlock Holmes. This new mystery is a tribute to *The Engineer's Thumb*. http://authl.it/aio

The Adventure of the Notable Bachelorette. A snobbish nobleman enters 221B Baker Street demanding the help in finding his much younger wife – a beautiful and spirited American from the West. Three days later the wife is accused of a vile crime. Now she comes to Sherlock Holmes seeking to prove her innocence. This new mystery was inspired by *The Adventure of the Noble Bachelor*. http://authl.it/aip

The Adventure of the Beryl Anarchists. A deeply distressed banker enters 221B Baker St. His safe has been robbed, and he is certain that his motorcycle-riding sons have betrayed him. Highly incriminating and embarrassing records of the financial and personal affairs of England's nobility are now in the hands of blackmailers. Then a young girl is murdered. A tribute to *The Adventure of the Beryl Coronet*. http://authl.it/aiq

The Adventure of the Coiffured Bitches. A beautiful young woman will soon inherit a lot of money. She disappears. Another young woman finds out far too much and, in desperation seeks help. Sherlock Holmes, Dr. Watson and Miss Violet Hunter must solve the mystery of the coiffured bitches and avoid the massive mastiff that could tear their throats out. A tribute to *The Adventure of the Copper Beeches*. http://authl.it/air

The Silver Horse, Braised. The greatest horse race of the century will take place at Epsom Downs. Millions have been bet. Owners, jockeys, grooms, and gamblers from across England and America arrive. Jockeys and horses are killed. Holmes fails to solve the crime until… This mystery is a tribute to *Silver Blaze* and the great racetrack stories of Damon Runyon. http://authl.it/ais

The Box of Cards. A brother and a sister from a strict religious family disappear. The parents are alarmed, but Scotland Yard says they are just off sowing their wild oats. A horrific, gruesome package arrives in the post, and it becomes clear that a terrible crime is in process. Sherlock Holmes is called in to help. A tribute to *The Cardboard Box.* http://authl.it/ait

The Yellow Farce. Sherlock Holmes is sent to Japan. The war between Russia and Japan is raging. Alliances between countries in these years before World War I are fragile, and any misstep could plunge the world into Armageddon. The wife of the British ambassador is suspected of being a Russian agent. Join Holmes and Watson as they travel around the world to Japan. Inspired by *The Yellow Face.* http://authl.it/akp

The Stock Market Murders. A young man's friend has gone missing. Two more bodies of young men turn up. All are tied to The City and to one of the greatest frauds ever visited upon the citizens of England. The story is based on the true story of James Whitaker Wright and is inspired by, *The Stock Broker's Clerk.* Any resemblance of the villain to a certain American political figure is entirely coincidental. http://authl.it/akq

The Glorious Yacht. On the night of April 12, 1912, off the coast of Newfoundland, one of the greatest disasters of all time took place – the Unsinkable Titanic struck an iceberg and sank with a horrendous loss of life. The news of the disaster leads Holmes and Watson to reminisce about one of their earliest adventures. It began as a sailing race and ended as a tale of murder, kidnapping, piracy, and survival through a tempest. A tribute to *The Gloria Scott.* http://authl.it/akr

A Most Grave Ritual. In 1649, King Charles I escaped and made a desperate run for Continent. Did he leave behind a vast fortune? The patriarch of an ancient Royalist family dies in the courtyard, and the locals believe that the headless ghost of the king did him in. The police accuse his son of murder. Sherlock Holmes is hired to exonerate the lad. A tribute to *The Musgrave Ritual.* http://authl.it/aks

The Spy Gate Liars. Dr. Watson receives an urgent telegram telling him that Sherlock Holmes is in France and near death. He rushes to aid his dear friend, only to find that what began as a doctor's house call has turned into yet another adventure as Sherlock Holmes races to keep an unknown ruthless murderer from dispatching yet another former German army officer. A tribute to *The Reigate Squires.* http://authl.it/akt

The Cuckold Man Colonel James Barclay needs the help of Sherlock Holmes. His exceptionally beautiful, but much younger, wife has disappeared, and foul play is suspected. Has she been kidnapped and held for ransom? Or is she in the clutches of a deviant monster? The story is a tribute not only to the original mystery, *The Crooked Man*, but also to the biblical story of King David and Bathsheba. http://authl.it/akv

The Impatient Dissidents. In March 1881, the Czar of Russia was assassinated by anarchists. That summer, an attempt was made to murder his daughter, Maria, the wife of England's Prince Alfred. A Russian Count is found dead in a hospital in London. Scotland Yard and the Home Office arrive at 221B and enlist the help of Sherlock Holmes to track down the killers and stop them. This new mystery is a tribute to *The Resident Patient.* http://authl.it/akw

The Grecian, Earned. This story picks up where *The Greek Interpreter* left off. The villains of that story were murdered in Budapest, and so Holmes and Watson set off in search of "the Grecian girl" to solve the mystery. What they discover is a massive plot involving the re-birth of the Olympic games in 1896 and a colorful cast of characters at home and on the Continent. http://authl.it/aia

The Three Rhodes Not Taken. Oxford University is famous for its passionate pursuit of learning. The Rhodes Scholarship has been recently established, and some men are prepared to lie, steal, slander, and, maybe murder, in the pursuit of it. Sherlock Holmes is called upon to track down a thief who has stolen vital documents pertaining to the winner of the scholarship, but what will he do when the prime suspect is found dead? A tribute to *The Three Students.* http://authl.it/al8

The Naval Knaves. On September 15, 1894, an anarchist attempted to bomb the Greenwich Observatory. He failed, but the attempt led Sherlock Holmes into an intricate web of spies, foreign naval officers, and a beautiful princess. Once again, suspicion landed on poor Percy Phelps, now working in a senior position in the Admiralty, and once again Holmes has to use both his powers of deduction and raw courage to not only rescue Percy but to prevent an unspeakable disaster. A tribute to *The Naval Treaty.* http://authl.it/aia

A Scandal in Trumplandia. NOT a new mystery but a political satire. The story is a parody of the much-loved original story, *A Scandal in Bohemia*, with the character of the King of Bohemia replaced by you-know-who. If you enjoy both political satire and Sherlock Holmes, you will get a chuckle out of this new story. http://authl.it/aig

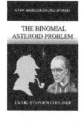

The Binomial Asteroid Problem. The deadly final encounter between Professor Moriarty and Sherlock Holmes took place at Reichenbach Falls. But when was their first encounter? This new story answers that question. What began a stolen Gladstone bag escalates into murder and more. This new story is a tribute to *The Adventure of the Final Problem.* http://authl.it/al1

The Adventure of Charlotte Europa Golderton. *Charles Augustus Milverton* was shot and sent to his just reward. But now another diabolical scheme of blackmail has emerged centered in the telegraph offices of the Royal Mail. It is linked to an archeological expedition whose director disappeared. Someone is prepared to murder to protect their ill-gotten gain and possibly steal a priceless treasure. Holmes is hired by not one but three women who need his help. http://authl.it/al7

The Mystery of 222 Baker Street. The body of a Scotland Yard inspector is found in a locked room in 222 Baker Street. There is no clue as to how he died, but he was murdered. Then another murder occurs in the very same room. Holmes and Watson might have to offer themselves as potential victims if the culprits are to be discovered. The story is a tribute to the original Sherlock Holmes story, *The Adventure of the Empty House.* http://authl.it/al3

The Adventure of the Norwood Rembrandt. A man facing execution appeals to Sherlock Holmes to save him. He claims that he is innocent. Holmes agrees to take on his case. Five years ago, he was convicted of the largest theft of art masterpieces in British history, and of murdering the butler who tried to stop him. Holmes and Watson have to find the real murderer and the missing works of art --- if the client is innocent after all. This new Sherlock Holmes mystery is a tribute to *The Adventure of the Norwood Builder* in the original Canon. http://authl.it/al4

The Horror of the Bastard's Villa. A Scottish clergyman and his faithful border collie visit 221B and tell a tale of a ghostly Banshee on the Isle of Skye. After the specter appeared, two people died. Holmes sends Watson on ahead to investigate and report. More terrifying horrors occur, and Sherlock Holmes must come and solve the awful mystery before more people are murdered. A tribute to the original story in the Canon, Arthur Conan Doyle's masterpiece, *The Hound of the Baskervilles.* http://authl.it/al2

The Dancer from the Dance. In 1909 the entire world of dance changed when Les Ballets Russes, under opened in Paris. They also made annual visits to the West End in London. Tragically, during their 1913 tour, two of their dancers are found murdered. Sherlock Holmes is brought into to find the murderer and prevent any more killings. The story adheres fairly closely to the history of ballet and is a tribute to the original story in the Canon, *The Adventure of the Dancing Men.* http://authl.it/al5

The Solitary Bicycle Thief. Remember Violet Smith, the beautiful young woman whom Sherlock Holmes and Dr. Watson rescued from a forced marriage, as recorded in *The Adventure of the Solitary Cyclist?* Ten years later she and Cyril reappear in 221B Baker Street with a strange tale of the theft of their bicycles. What on the surface seemed like a trifle turns out to be the door that leads Sherlock Holmes into a web of human trafficking, espionage, blackmail, and murder. A new and powerful cabal of master criminals has formed in London, and they will stop at nothing, not even the murder of an innocent foreign student, to extend the hold on the criminal underworld of London. http://authl.it/al6

The Adventure of the Prioress's Tale. The senior field hockey team from an elite girls' school goes to Dover for a beach holiday … and disappears. Have they been abducted into white slavery? Did they run off to Paris? Are they being held for ransom? Can Sherlock Holmes find them in time? Holmes, Watson, Lestrade, the Prioress of the school, and a new gang of Irregulars must find them before something terrible happens. A tribute to *The Adventure of the Priory School in the Canon.* http://authl.it/apv

The Adventure of Mrs. J.L. Heber. A mad woman is murdering London bachelors by driving a railway spike through their heads. Scotland Yard demands that Sherlock Holmes help them find and stop a crazed murderess who is re-enacting the biblical murders by Jael. Holmes agrees and finds that revenge is being taken for deeds treachery and betrayal that took place ten years ago in the Rocky Mountains of Canada. Holmes, Watson, and Lestrade must move quickly before more men and women lose their lives. The story is a tribute to the original Sherlock Holmes story, *The Adventure of Black Peter.* http://authl.it/arr

The Return of Napoleon. In October 1805, Napoleon's fleet was defeated in the Battle of Trafalgar. Now his ghost has returned to England for the centenary of the battle, intent on wreaking revenge on the descendants of Admiral Horatio Nelson and on all of England. The mother of the great-great-grandchildren of Admiral Nelson contacts Sherlock Holmes and asks him to come to her home, Victory Manor, in Gravesend to protect the Nelson Collection. The invaluable collection of artifacts is to be displayed during the one-hundredth anniversary celebrations of the Battle of Trafalgar. First, Dr. Watson comes to the manor and he meets not only the lovely children but also finds that something apparently supernatural is going on. Holmes assumes that some mad Frenchmen, intent on avenging Napoleon, are conspiring to wreak havoc on England and possibly threatening the children. Watson believes that something terrifying and occult may be at work. Neither is prepared for the true target of the Napoleonists, or of the Emperor's ghost. http://authl.it/at4

The Adventure of the Pinched Palimpsest. At Oxford University, an influential professor has been proselytizing for anarchism. Three naive students fall for his doctrines and decide to engage in direct action by stealing priceless artifacts from the British Museum, returning them to the oppressed people from whom their colonial masters stole them. In the midst of their caper, a museum guard is shot dead and they are charged with the murder. After being persuaded by a vulnerable friend of the students, Sherlock Holmes agrees to take on the case. He soon discovers that no one involved is telling the complete truth. Join Holmes and Watson as they race from London to Oxford, then to Cambridge and finally up to a remote village in Scotland and seek to discover the clues that are tied to an obscure medieval palimpsest. http://authl.it/ax0

Contributions to The Great Game of Sherlockian Scholarship

 ***Sherlock and Barack.*** This is NOT a new Sherlock Holmes Mystery. It is a Sherlockian research monograph. Why did Barack Obama win in November 2012? Why did Mitt Romney lose? Pundits and political scientists have offered countless reasons. This book reveals the truth - The Sherlock Holmes Factor. Had it not been for Sherlock Holmes, Mitt Romney would be president. http://authl.it/aid

 ***From The Beryl Coronet to Vimy Ridge.*** This is NOT a New Sherlock Holmes Mystery. It is a monograph of Sherlockian research. This new monograph in the Great Game of Sherlockian scholarship argues that there was a Sherlock Holmes factor in the causes of World War I... and that it is secretly revealed in the *roman a clef* story that we know as *The Adventure of the Beryl Coronet*. http://authl.it/ali

Reverend Ezekiel Black Mystery Stories.
The Sherlock Holmes of the American West

A Scarlet Trail of Murder. At ten o'clock on Sunday morning, the twenty-second of October, 1882, in an abandoned house in the West Bottom of Kansas City, a fellow named Jasper Harrison did not wake up. His inability to do was the result of his having had his throat cut. The Reverend Mr. Ezekiel Black, a part-time Methodist minister, and an itinerant US Marshall is called in. This original western mystery was inspired by the great Sherlock Holmes classic, *A Study in Scarlet.* http://authl.it/alg

The Brand of the Flying Four. This case all began one quiet evening in a room in Kansas City. A few weeks later, a gruesome murder, took place in Denver. By the time Rev. Black had solved the mystery, justice, of the frontier variety, not the courtroom, had been meted out. The story is inspired by *The Sign of the Four* by Arthur Conan Doyle, and like that story, it combines murder most foul, and romance most enticing. http://authl.it/alh

www.SherlockHolmesMystery.com

Collection Sets for eBooks and paperback are available at *40% off the price of buying them separately.*

Collection One http://authl.it/al9

The Sign of the Tooth
The Hudson Valley Mystery
A Case of Identity Theft
The Bald-Headed Trust
Studying Scarlet
The Mystery of the Five Oranges

Collection Two http://authl.it/ala

A Sandal from East Anglia
The Man Who Was Twisted But Hip
The Blue Belt Buckle
The Spectred Bat

Collection Three http://authl.it/alb

The Engineer's Mom
The Notable Bachelorette
The Beryl Anarchists
The Coiffured Bitches

Collection Four http://authl.it/alc

The Silver Horse, Braised
The Box of Cards
The Yellow Farce
The Three Rhodes Not Taken

Collection Five http://authl.it/ald

The Stock Market Murders
The Glorious Yacht
The Most Grave Ritual
The Spy Gate Liars

Collection Six http://authl.it/ale

The Cuckold Man
The Impatient Dissidents
The Grecian, Earned
The Naval Knaves

Collection Seven http://authl.it/alf

The Binomial Asteroid Problem
The Mystery of 222 Baker Street
The Adventure of Charlotte Europa Golderton
The Adventure of the Norwood Rembrandt

Collection Eight http://authl.it/at3

The Dancer from the Dance
The Adventure of the Prioress's Tale
The Adventure of Mrs. J. L. Heber
The Solitary Bicycle Thief

Super Collections A and B

30 New Sherlock Holmes Mysteries.

http://authl.it/aiw, http://authl.it/aix

The perfect ebooks for readers who can only borrow one book a month from Amazon

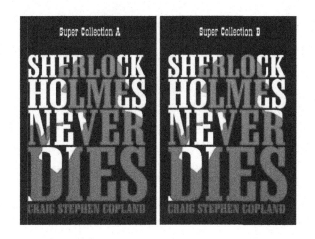

www.SherlockHolmesMystery.com

The Adventure of Charles Augustus Milverton

The Original Sherlock Holmes Story

Arthur Conan Doyle

The Adventure of Charles Augustus Milverton

IT IS YEARS since the incidents of which I speak took place, and yet it is with diffidence that I allude to them. For a long time, even with the utmost discretion and reticence, it would have been impossible to make the facts public; but now the principal person concerned is beyond the reach of human law, and with due suppression the story may be told in such fashion as to injure no one. It records an absolutely unique experience in the career both of Mr. Sherlock Holmes and of myself. The reader will excuse me if I conceal the date or any other fact by which he might trace the actual occurrence.

We had been out for one of our evening rambles, Holmes and I, and had returned about six o'clock on a cold, frosty winter's evening. As Holmes turned up the lamp the light fell upon a card on the table. He glanced at it, and then, with an ejaculation of disgust, threw it on the floor. I picked it up and read:—

CHARLES AUGUSTUS MILVERTON,
APPLEDORE TOWERS,
AGENT. HAMPSTEAD.

"Who is he?" I asked.

"The worst man in London," Holmes answered, as he sat down and stretched his legs before the fire. "Is anything on the back of the card?"

I turned it over.

"Will call at 6.30—C.A.M.," I read.

"Hum! He's about due. Do you feel a creeping, shrinking sensation, Watson, when you stand before the serpents in the Zoo and see the slithery, gliding, venomous creatures, with their deadly eyes and wicked, flattened faces? Well, that's how Milverton impresses me. I've had to do with fifty murderers in my career, but the worst of them never gave me the repulsion which I have for this fellow. And yet I can't get out of doing business with him—indeed, he is here at my invitation."

"But who is he?"

"I'll tell you, Watson. He is the king of all the blackmailers. Heaven help the man, and still more the woman, whose secret and reputation come into the power of Milverton. With a smiling face and a heart of marble he will squeeze and squeeze until he has drained them dry. The fellow is a genius in his way, and would have made his mark in some more savoury trade. His method is as follows: He allows it to be known that he is prepared to pay very high sums for letters which compromise people of wealth or position. He receives these wares not only from treacherous valets or maids, but frequently from genteel ruffians who have gained the confidence and affection of trusting women. He deals with no niggard hand. I happen to know that he paid seven hundred pounds to a footman for a note two lines in length, and that the ruin of a noble family was the result. Everything which is in the market goes to Milverton, and there are hundreds in this great city who turn white at his name. No one knows where his grip may fall, for he is far too rich and far too cunning to work from hand to mouth. He will hold a card back for years in order to play it at the moment when the stake is best worth winning. I have said that he is the worst man in London, and I would ask you how could one compare the ruffian who in hot blood bludgeons his mate with this man, who methodically and at his leisure tortures the soul and wrings the nerves in order to add to his already swollen money-bags?"

I had seldom heard my friend speak with such intensity of feeling.

"But surely," said I, "the fellow must be within the grasp of the law?"

"Technically, no doubt, but practically not. What would it profit a woman, for example, to get him a few months' imprisonment if her own ruin must immediately follow? His victims dare not hit back. If ever he blackmailed an innocent person, then, indeed, we should have him; but he is as cunning as the Evil One. No, no; we must find other ways to fight him."

"And why is he here?"

"Because an illustrious client has placed her piteous case in my hands. It is the Lady Eva Brackwell, the most beautiful DEBUTANTE of last season. She is to be married in a fortnight to the Earl of Dovercourt. This fiend has several imprudent letters—imprudent, Watson, nothing worse—which were written to an impecunious young squire in the country. They would suffice to break off the match. Milverton will send the letters to the Earl unless a large sum of money is paid him. I have been commissioned to meet him, and—to make the best terms I can."

At that instant there was a clatter and a rattle in the street below. Looking down I saw a stately carriage and pair, the brilliant lamps gleaming on the glossy haunches of the noble chestnuts. A footman opened the door, and a small, stout man in a shaggy astrachan overcoat descended. A minute later he was in the room.

Charles Augustus Milverton was a man of fifty, with a large, intellectual head, a round, plump, hairless face, a perpetual frozen smile, and two keen grey eyes, which gleamed brightly from behind broad, golden-rimmed glasses. There was something of Mr. Pickwick's benevolence in his appearance, marred only by the insincerity of the fixed smile and by the hard glitter of those restless and penetrating eyes. His voice was as smooth and suave as his countenance, as he advanced with a plump little hand extended, murmuring his regret for having missed us at his first visit. Holmes disregarded the outstretched hand and looked at him with a face of granite. Milverton's smile broadened; he shrugged his shoulders, removed his overcoat, folded it with great deliberation over the back of a chair, and then took a seat.

"This gentleman?" said he, with a wave in my direction. "Is it discreet? Is it right?"

"Dr. Watson is my friend and partner."

"Very good, Mr. Holmes. It is only in your client's interests that I protested. The matter is so very delicate—"

"Dr. Watson has already heard of it."

"Then we can proceed to business. You say that you are acting for Lady Eva. Has she empowered you to accept my terms?"

"What are your terms?"

"Seven thousand pounds."

"And the alternative?"

"My dear sir, it is painful for me to discuss it; but if the money is not paid on the 14th there certainly will be no marriage on the 18th." His insufferable smile was more complacent than ever.

Holmes thought for a little.

"You appear to me," he said, at last, "to be taking matters too much for granted. I am, of course, familiar with the contents of these letters. My client will certainly do what I may advise. I shall counsel her to tell her future husband the whole story and to trust to his generosity."

Milverton chuckled.

"You evidently do not know the Earl," said he.

From the baffled look upon Holmes's face I could see clearly that he did.

"What harm is there in the letters?" he asked.

"They are sprightly—very sprightly," Milverton answered. "The lady was a charming correspondent. But I can assure you that the Earl of Dovercourt would fail to appreciate them. However, since you think otherwise, we will let it rest at that. It is purely a matter of business. If you think that it is in the best interests of your client that these letters should be placed in the hands of the Earl, then you would indeed be foolish to pay so large a sum of money to regain them." He rose and seized his astrachan coat.

Holmes was grey with anger and mortification.

"Wait a little," he said. "You go too fast. We would certainly make every effort to avoid scandal in so delicate a matter."

Milverton relapsed into his chair.

"I was sure that you would see it in that light," he purred.

"At the same time," Holmes continued, "Lady Eva is not a wealthy woman. I assure you that two thousand pounds would be a drain upon her resources, and that the sum you name is utterly beyond her power. I beg, therefore, that you will moderate your demands, and that you will return the letters at the price I indicate, which is, I assure you, the highest that you can get."

Milverton's smile broadened and his eyes twinkled humorously.

"I am aware that what you say is true about the lady's resources," said he. "At the same time, you must admit that the occasion of a lady's marriage is a very suitable time for her friends and relatives to make some little effort upon her behalf. They may hesitate as to an acceptable wedding present. Let me assure them that this little bundle of letters would give more joy than all the candelabra and butter-dishes in London."

"It is impossible," said Holmes.

"Dear me, dear me, how unfortunate!" cried Milverton, taking out a bulky pocket-book. "I cannot help thinking that ladies are ill-advised in not making an effort. Look at this!" He held up a little note with a coat-of-arms upon the envelope. "That belongs to—well, perhaps it is hardly fair to tell the name until to-morrow morning. But at that time it will be in the hands of the lady's husband. And all because she will not find a beggarly sum which she could get by turning her diamonds into paste. It IS such a pity. Now, you remember the sudden end of the engagement between the Honourable Miss Miles and Colonel Dorking? Only two days before the wedding there was a paragraph in the MORNING POST to say that it was all off. And why? It is almost incredible, but the absurd sum of twelve hundred pounds would have settled the whole question. Is it not pitiful? And here I find you, a man of sense, boggling about terms when your client's future and honour are at stake. You surprise me, Mr. Holmes."

"What I say is true," Holmes answered. "The money cannot be found. Surely it is better for you to take the substantial sum which I offer than to ruin this woman's career, which can profit you in no way?"

"There you make a mistake, Mr. Holmes. An exposure would profit me indirectly to a considerable extent. I have eight or ten similar cases maturing. If it was circulated among them that I had made a severe example of the Lady Eva I should find all of them much more open to reason. You see my point?"

Holmes sprang from his chair.

"Get behind him, Watson! Don't let him out! Now, sir, let us see the contents of that note-book."

Milverton had glided as quick as a rat to the side of the room, and stood with his back against the wall.

"Mr. Holmes, Mr. Holmes," he said, turning the front of his coat and exhibiting the butt of a large revolver, which projected from the inside pocket. "I have been expecting you to do something original. This has been done so often, and what good has ever come from it? I assure you that I am armed to the teeth, and I am perfectly prepared to use my weapons, knowing that the law will support me. Besides, your supposition that I would bring the letters here in a note-book is entirely mistaken. I would do nothing so foolish. And now, gentlemen, I have one or two little interviews this evening, and it is a long drive to Hampstead." He stepped forward, took up his coat, laid his hand on his revolver, and turned to the door. I picked up a chair, but Holmes shook his head and I laid it down again. With bow, a smile, and a twinkle Milverton was out of the room, and a few moments after we heard the slam of the carriage door and the rattle of the wheels as he drove away.

Holmes sat motionless by the fire, his hands buried deep in his trouser pockets, his chin sunk upon his breast, his eyes fixed upon the glowing embers. For half an hour he was silent and still. Then, with the gesture of a man who has taken his decision, he sprang to his feet and passed into his bedroom. A little later a rakish young workman with a goatee beard and a swagger lit his clay pipe at the lamp before descending into the street. "I'll be back some time, Watson," said he, and vanished into the night. I understood that he had opened his campaign against Charles Augustus Milverton; but I little dreamed the strange shape which that campaign was destined to take.

For some days Holmes came and went at all hours in this attire, but beyond a remark that his time was spent at Hampstead, and that it was not wasted, I knew nothing of what he was doing. At last, however, on a wild, tempestuous evening, when the wind screamed and rattled against the windows, he returned from his last expedition, and having removed his disguise he sat before the fire and laughed heartily in his silent inward fashion.

"You would not call me a marrying man, Watson?"

"No, indeed!"

"You'll be interested to hear that I am engaged."

"My dear fellow! I congrat—"

"To Milverton's housemaid."

"Good heavens, Holmes!"

"I wanted information, Watson."

"Surely you have gone too far?"

"It was a most necessary step. I am a plumber with a rising business, Escott by name. I have walked out with her each evening, and I have talked with her. Good heavens, those talks! However, I have got all I wanted. I know Milverton's house as I know the palm of my hand."

"But the girl, Holmes?"

He shrugged his shoulders.

"You can't help it, my dear Watson. You must play your cards as best you can when such a stake is on the table. However, I rejoice to say that I have a hated rival who will certainly cut me out the instant that my back is turned. What a splendid night it is!"

"You like this weather?"

"It suits my purpose. Watson, I mean to burgle Milverton's house to-night."

I had a catching of the breath, and my skin went cold at the words, which were slowly uttered in a tone of concentrated resolution. As a flash of lightning in the night shows up in an instant every detail of a wide landscape, so at one glance I seemed to see every possible result of such an action—the detection, the capture, the honoured career ending in irreparable failure and disgrace, my friend himself lying at the mercy of the odious Milverton.

"For Heaven's sake, Holmes, think what you are doing," I cried.

"My dear fellow, I have given it every consideration. I am never precipitate in my actions, nor would I adopt so energetic and indeed so dangerous a course if any other were possible. Let us look at the matter clearly and fairly. I suppose that you will admit that the action is morally justifiable, though technically criminal. To burgle his house is no more than to forcibly take his pocket-book—an action in which you were prepared to aid me."

I turned it over in my mind.

"Yes," I said; "it is morally justifiable so long as our object is to take no articles save those which are used for an illegal purpose."

"Exactly. Since it is morally justifiable I have only to consider the question of personal risk. Surely a gentleman should not lay much stress upon this when a lady is in most desperate need of his help?"

"You will be in such a false position."

"Well, that is part of the risk. There is no other possible way of regaining these letters. The unfortunate lady has not the money, and there are none of her people in whom she could confide. To-morrow is the last day of grace, and unless we can get the letters to-night this villain will be as good as his word and will bring about her ruin. I must, therefore, abandon my client to her fate or I must play this last card. Between ourselves, Watson, it's a sporting duel between this fellow Milverton and me. He had, as you saw, the best of the first exchanges; but my self-respect and my reputation are concerned to fight it to a finish."

"Well, I don't like it; but I suppose it must be," said I. "When do we start?"

"You are not coming."

"Then you are not going," said I. "I give you my word of honour —and I never broke it in my life—that I will take a cab straight to the police-station and give you away unless you let me share this adventure with you." two men looking into a shop window

"You can't help me."

"How do you know that? You can't tell what may happen. Anyway, my resolution is taken. Other people beside you have self-respect and even reputations."

Holmes had looked annoyed, but his brow cleared, and he clapped me on the shoulder.

"Well, well, my dear fellow, be it so. We have shared the same room for some years, and it would be amusing if we ended by sharing the same cell. You know, Watson, I don't mind confessing to you that I have always had an idea that I would have made a highly efficient criminal. This is the chance of my lifetime in that direction. See here!" He took a neat little leather case out of a drawer, and opening it he exhibited a number of shining instruments. "This is a first-class, up-to-date burgling kit, with nickel-plated jemmy, diamond-tipped glass-cutter, adaptable keys, and every modern improvement which the march of civilization demands. Here, too, is my dark lantern. Everything is in order. Have you a pair of silent shoes?"

"I have rubber-soled tennis shoes."

"Excellent. And a mask?"

"I can make a couple out of black silk."

"I can see that you have a strong natural turn for this sort of thing. Very good; do you make the masks. We shall have some cold supper before we start. It is now nine-thirty. At eleven we shall drive as far as Church Row. It is a quarter of an hour's walk from there to Appledore Towers. We shall be at work before midnight. Milverton is a heavy sleeper and retires punctually at ten-thirty. With any luck we should be back here by two, with the Lady Eva's letters in my pocket."

Holmes and I put on our dress-clothes, so that we might appear to be two theatre-goers homeward bound. In Oxford Street we picked up a hansom and drove to an address in Hampstead. Here we paid off our cab, and with our great-coats buttoned up, for it was bitterly cold and the wind seemed to blow through us, we walked along the edge of the Heath.

"It's a business that needs delicate treatment," said Holmes. "These documents are contained in a safe in the fellow's study, and the study is the ante-room of his bed-chamber. On the other hand, like all these stout, little men who do themselves well, he is a plethoric sleeper. Agatha—

that's my FIANCEE—says it is a joke in the servants' hall that it's impossible to wake the master. He has a secretary who is devoted to his interests and never budges from the study all day. That's why we are going at night. Then he has a beast of a dog which roams the garden. I met Agatha late the last two evenings, and she locks the brute up so as to give me a clear run. This is the house, this big one in its own grounds. Through the gate—now to the right among the laurels. We might put on our masks here, I think. You see, there is not a glimmer of light in any of the windows, and everything is working splendidly."

With our black silk face-coverings, which turned us into two of the most truculent figures in London, we stole up to the silent, gloomy house. A sort of tiled veranda extended along one side of it, lined by several windows and two doors.

"That's his bedroom," Holmes whispered. "This door opens straight into the study. It would suit us best, but it is bolted as well as locked, and we should make too much noise getting in. Come round here. There's a greenhouse which opens into the drawing-room."

The place was locked, but Holmes removed a circle of glass and turned the key from the inside. An instant afterwards he had closed the door behind us, and we had become felons in the eyes of the law. The thick, warm air of the conservatory and the rich, choking fragrance of exotic plants took us by the throat. He seized my hand in the darkness and led me swiftly past banks of shrubs which brushed against our faces. Holmes had remarkable powers, carefully cultivated, of seeing in the dark. Still holding my hand in one of his he opened a door, and I was vaguely conscious that we had entered a large room in which a cigar had been smoked not long before. He felt his way among the furniture, opened another door, and closed it behind us. Putting out my hand I felt several coats hanging from the wall, and I understood that I was in a passage. We passed along it, and Holmes very gently opened a door upon the right-hand side. Something rushed out at us and my heart sprang into my mouth, but I could have laughed when I realized that it was the cat. A fire was burning in this new room, and again the air was heavy with tobacco smoke. Holmes entered on tiptoe, waited for me to follow, and then very gently closed the door. We were in Milverton's study, and a PORTIERE at the farther side showed the entrance to his bedroom.

It was a good fire, and the room was illuminated by it. Near the door I saw the gleam of an electric switch, but it was unnecessary, even if it had been safe, to turn it on. At one side of the fireplace was a heavy curtain, which covered the bay window we had seen from outside. On the other side was the door which communicated with the veranda. A desk stood in the centre, with a turning chair of shining red leather. Opposite was a large bookcase, with a marble bust of Athene on the top. In the corner between the bookcase and the wall there stood a tall green safe, the firelight flashing back from the polished brass knobs upon its face. Holmes stole across and looked at it. Then he crept to the door of the bedroom, and stood with slanting head listening intently. No sound came from within. Meanwhile it had struck me that it would be wise to secure our retreat through the outer door, so I examined it. To my amazement it was neither locked nor bolted! I touched Holmes on the arm, and he turned his masked face in that direction. I saw him start, and he was evidently as surprised as I.

"I don't like it," he whispered, putting his lips to my very ear. "I can't quite make it out. Anyhow, we have no time to lose."

"Can I do anything?"

"Yes; stand by the door. If you hear anyone come, bolt it on the inside, and we can get away as we came. If they come the other way, we can get through the door if our job is done, or hide behind these window curtains if it is not. Do you understand?"

I nodded and stood by the door. My first feeling of fear had passed away, and I thrilled now with a keener zest than I had ever enjoyed when we were the defenders of the law instead of its defiers. The high object of our mission, the consciousness that it was unselfish and chivalrous, the villainous character of our opponent, all added to the sporting interest of the adventure. Far from feeling guilty, I rejoiced and exulted in our dangers. With a glow of admiration I watched Holmes unrolling his case of instruments and choosing his tool with the calm, scientific accuracy of a surgeon who performs a delicate operation. I knew that the opening of safes was a particular hobby with him, and I understood the joy which it gave him to be confronted with this green and gold monster, the dragon which held in its maw the reputations of many fair ladies. Turning up the cuffs of his dress-coat—he had placed his overcoat on a chair—Holmes laid out two drills, a jemmy, and several skeleton keys. I stood at the centre door with my eyes glancing at each of the others, ready for any emergency; though, indeed, my plans were somewhat vague as to what I should do if we were interrupted. For half an hour Holmes worked with concentrated energy, laying down one tool, picking up another, handling each with the strength and delicacy of the trained mechanic. Finally I heard a click, the broad green door swung open, and inside I had a glimpse of a number of paper packets, each tied, sealed, and inscribed. Holmes picked one out, but it was hard to read by the flickering fire, and he drew out his little dark lantern, for it was too dangerous, with Milverton in the next room, to switch on the electric light. Suddenly I saw him halt, listen intently, and then in an instant he had swung the door of the safe to, picked up his coat, stuffed his tools into the pockets, and darted behind the window curtain, motioning me to do the same.

It was only when I had joined him there that I heard what had alarmed his quicker senses. There was a noise somewhere within the house. A door slammed in the distance. Then a confused, dull murmur broke itself into the measured thud of heavy footsteps rapidly approaching. They were in the passage outside the room. They paused at the door. The door opened. There was a sharp snick as the electric light was turned on. The door closed once more, and the pungent reek of a strong cigar was borne to our nostrils. Then the footsteps continued backwards and forwards, backwards and forwards, within a few yards of us. Finally, there was a creak from a chair, and the footsteps ceased. Then a key clicked in a lock and I heard the rustle of papers.

So far I had not dared to look out, but now I gently parted the division of the curtains in front of me and peeped through. From the pressure of Holmes's shoulder against mine I knew that he was sharing my observations. Right in front of us, and almost within our reach, was the broad, rounded back of Milverton. It was evident that we had entirely miscalculated his movements, that he had never been to his bedroom, but that he had been sitting up in some smoking or billiard room in the farther wing of the house, the windows of which we had not seen. His broad, grizzled head, with its shining patch of baldness, was in the immediate foreground of our vision. He was leaning far back in the red leather chair, his legs outstretched, a long black cigar projecting at an angle from his mouth. He wore a semi-military smoking jacket, claret-coloured, with a black velvet collar. In his hand he held a long legal document, which he was reading in an indolent fashion, blowing rings of tobacco smoke from his lips as he did so. There was no promise of a speedy departure in his composed bearing and his comfortable attitude.

I felt Holmes's hand steal into mine and give me a reassuring shake, as if to say that the situation was within his powers and that he was easy in his mind. I was not sure whether he had seen what was only too obvious from my position, that the door of the safe was imperfectly closed, and that Milverton might at any moment observe it. In my own mind I had determined that if I were sure, from the rigidity of his gaze, that it had caught his eye, I would at once spring out, throw my great-coat over his head, pinion him, and leave the rest to Holmes. But Milverton never looked up. He was languidly interested by the papers in his hand, and page after page was turned as he followed the argument of the lawyer. At least, I thought, when he has finished the document and the cigar he will go to his room; but before he had reached the end of either there came a remarkable development which turned our thoughts into quite another channel.

Several times I had observed that Milverton looked at his watch, and once he had risen and sat down again, with a gesture of impatience. The idea, however, that he might have an appointment at so strange an hour never occurred to me until a faint sound reached my ears from the veranda outside. Milverton dropped his papers and sat rigid in his chair. The sound was repeated, and then there came a gentle tap at the door. Milverton rose and opened it.

"Well," said he, curtly, "you are nearly half an hour late."

So this was the explanation of the unlocked door and of the nocturnal vigil of Milverton. There was the gentle rustle of a woman's dress. I had closed the slit between the curtains as Milverton's face had turned in our direction, but now I ventured very carefully to open it once more. He had resumed his seat, the cigar still projecting at an insolent angle from the corner of his mouth. In front of him, in the full glare of the electric light, there stood a tall, slim, dark woman, a veil over her face, a mantle drawn round her chin. Her breath came quick and fast, and every inch of the lithe figure was quivering with strong emotion.

"Well," said Milverton, "you've made me lose a good night's rest, my dear. I hope you'll prove worth it. You couldn't come any other time—eh?"

The woman shook her head.

"Well, if you couldn't you couldn't. If the Countess is a hard mistress you have your chance to get level with her now. Bless the girl, what are you shivering about? That's right! Pull yourself together! Now, let us get down to business." He took a note from the drawer of his desk. "You say that you have five letters which compromise the Countess d'Albert. You want to sell them. I want to buy them. So far so good. It only remains to fix a price. I should want to inspect the letters, of course. If they are really good specimens— Great heavens, is it you?"

The woman without a word had raised her veil and dropped the mantle from her chin. It was a dark, handsome, clear-cut face which confronted Milverton, a face with a curved nose, strong, dark eyebrows shading hard, glittering eyes, and a straight, thin-lipped mouth set in a dangerous smile.

"It is I," she said; "the woman whose life you have ruined."

Milverton laughed, but fear vibrated in his voice. "You were so very obstinate," said he. "Why did you drive me to such extremities? I assure you I wouldn't hurt a fly of my own accord, but every man has his business, and what was I to do? I put the price well within your means. You would not pay."

"So you sent the letters to my husband, and he—the noblest gentleman that ever lived, a man whose boots I was never worthy to lace—he broke his gallant heart and died. You remember that last night when I came through that door

I begged and prayed you for mercy, and you laughed in my face as you are trying to laugh now, only your coward heart cannot keep your lips from twitching? Yes, you never thought to see me here again, but it was that night which taught me how I could meet you face to face, and alone. Well, Charles Milverton, what have you to say?"

"Don't imagine that you can bully me," said he, rising to his feet. "I have only to raise my voice, and I could call my servants and have you arrested. But I will make allowance for your natural anger. Leave the room at once as you came, and I will say no more."

The woman stood with her hand buried in her bosom, and the same deadly smile on her thin lips.

"You will ruin no more lives as you ruined mine. You will wring no more hearts as you wrung mine. I will free the world of a poisonous thing. Take that, you hound, and that!—and that! —and that!"

She had drawn a little, gleaming revolver, and emptied barrel after barrel into Milverton's body, the muzzle within two feet of his shirt front. He shrank away and then fell forward upon the table, coughing furiously and clawing among the papers. Then he staggered to his feet, received another shot, and rolled upon the floor. "You've done me," he cried, and lay still. The woman looked at him intently and ground her heel into his upturned face. She looked again, but there was no sound or movement. I heard a sharp rustle, the night air blew into the heated room, and the avenger was gone.

No interference upon our part could have saved the man from his fate; but as the woman poured bullet after bullet into Milverton's shrinking body I was about to spring out, when I felt Holmes's cold, strong grasp upon my wrist. I understood the whole argument of that firm, restraining grip—that it was no affair of ours; that justice had overtaken a villain; that we had our own duties and our own objects which were not to be lost sight of. But hardly had the woman rushed from the room when Holmes, with swift, silent steps, was over at the other door. He turned the key in the lock. At the same instant we heard voices in the house and the sound of hurrying feet. The revolver shots had roused the household. With perfect coolness Holmes slipped across to the safe, filled his two arms with bundles of letters, and poured them all into the fire. Again and again he did it, until the safe was empty. Someone turned the handle and beat upon the outside of the door. Holmes looked swiftly round. The letter which had been the messenger of death for Milverton lay, all mottled with his blood, upon the table. Holmes tossed it in among the blazing papers. Then he drew the key from the outer door, passed through after me, and locked it on the outside. "This way, Watson," said he; "we can scale the garden wall in this direction."

I could not have believed that an alarm could have spread so swiftly. Looking back, the huge house was one blaze of light. The front door was open, and figures were rushing down the drive. The whole garden was alive with people, and one fellow raised a view-halloa as we emerged from the veranda and followed hard at our heels. Holmes seemed to know the ground perfectly, and he threaded his way swiftly among a plantation of small trees, I close at his heels, and our foremost pursuer panting behind us. It was a six-foot wall which barred our path, but he sprang to the top and over. As I did the same I felt the hand of the man behind me grab at my ankle; but I kicked myself free and scrambled over a glass-strewn coping. I fell upon my face among some bushes; but Holmes had me on my feet in an instant, and together we dashed away across the huge expanse of Hampstead Heath. We had run two miles, I suppose, before Holmes at last halted and listened intently. All was absolute silence behind us. We had shaken off our pursuers and were safe.

We had breakfasted and were smoking our morning pipe on the day after the remarkable experience which I have recorded when Mr. Lestrade, of Scotland Yard, very solemn and impressive, was ushered into our modest sitting-room.

"Good morning, Mr. Holmes," said he; "good morning. May I ask if you are very busy just now?"

"Not too busy to listen to you."

"I thought that, perhaps, if you had nothing particular on hand, you might care to assist us in a most remarkable case which occurred only last night at Hampstead."

"Dear me!" said Holmes. "What was that?"

"A murder—a most dramatic and remarkable murder. I know how keen you are upon these things, and I would take it as a great favour if you would step down to Appledore Towers and give us the benefit of your advice. It is no ordinary crime. We have had our eyes upon this Mr. Milverton for some time, and, between ourselves, he was a bit of a villain. He is known to have held papers which he used for blackmailing purposes. These papers have all been burned by the murderers. No article of value was taken, as it is probable that the criminals were men of good position, whose sole object was to prevent social exposure."

"Criminals!" said Holmes. "Plural!"

"Yes, there were two of them. They were, as nearly as possible, captured red-handed. We have their foot-marks, we have their description; it's ten to one that we trace them. The first fellow was a bit too active, but the second was caught by the under-gardener and only got away after a struggle. He was a middle-sized, strongly-built man—square jaw, thick neck, moustache, a mask over his eyes."

"That's rather vague," said Sherlock Holmes. "Why, it might be a description of Watson!"

"It's true," said the inspector, with much amusement. "It might be a description of Watson."

"Well, I am afraid I can't help you, Lestrade," said Holmes. "The fact is that I knew this fellow Milverton, that I considered him one of the most dangerous men in London, and that I think there are certain crimes which the law cannot touch, and which therefore, to some extent, justify private revenge. No, it's no use arguing. I have made up my mind. My sympathies are with the criminals rather than with the victim, and I will not handle this case."

Holmes had not said one word to me about the tragedy which we had witnessed, but I observed all the morning that he was in his most thoughtful mood, and he gave me the impression, from his vacant eyes and his abstracted manner, of a man who is striving to recall something to his memory. We were in the middle of our lunch when he suddenly sprang to his feet. "By Jove, Watson; I've got it!" he cried. "Take your hat! Come with me!" He hurried at his top speed down Baker Street and along Oxford Street, until we had almost reached Regent Circus. Here on the left hand there stands a shop window filled with photographs of the celebrities and beauties of the day. Holmes's eyes fixed themselves upon

one of them, and following his gaze I saw the picture of a regal and stately lady in Court dress, with a high diamond tiara upon her noble head. I looked at that delicately-curved nose, at the marked eyebrows, at the straight mouth, and the strong little chin beneath it. Then I caught my breath as I read the time-honoured title of the great nobleman and statesman whose wife she had been. My eyes met those of Holmes, and he put his finger to his lips as we turned away from the window.

Made in United States
Orlando, FL
28 May 2024

47277835R00124